Beautiful TRAGEDIES IV

Curated by

Xtina Marie

www.hellboundbookspublishing.com

Contents:

Introduction
Candace Nola

I've long believed that poetry was the truest and most vulnerable form of expression, even as a young child there was something about poetry that stuck with me longer than any story ever did. The cadence of the words, the emotional pull, the tone and rhythms found within, most of it haunting, the darkest of it reverberating deep in my core where the hurt grows and festers like open wounds. Poetry speaks to your soul, or at least it speaks to mine.

The haunting verses of *The Raven, The Bells*, or *Annabel Lee* by Poe impacted me on a fundamental level. The loneliness of Emily Dickinson, the intelligence, trauma, and heartache of Phillis Wheatley, the music found within the words of Langston Hughes, and the sheer power, emotion, and truth within every verse Maya Angelou has ever written. These are the poets that raised me, that changed me and taught me how it was done. The feelings their words stirred within me are the same feelings that I hope to bring to others that read my work.

Reading Beautiful Tragedies, IV, reminded me that I am not alone anymore. That I am not the only one that feels things on such a deep visceral level, that understands what it means to bleed on the page, that gets chills when the cadence hits just right. I was honored to be asked to write for this anthology but even more flattered when I was asked to write the introduction for it as well.

The sheer amount of pain and heartache, grief and loss, love and longing that coat these pages is staggering as is the incredible wealth of talent that penned these verses for your reading pleasure. The poets, these incredible poets showcased in Beautiful Tragedies, remind us all of what it's like to feel our humanity again; to love, to lose, to grieve, to rejoice, and to mourn, at a time when the world needs it most.

Candace Nola, author of Unmasked
October 2025

Feed Him Clementines
Amanda Mitzel

If you're asking me if I killed a snake
yes I did and I feel terrible about it
He was ribboning across the road
as I drove home from the Clermont Target—
the store the road the everything
on top of orange groves razed to the ground
in a fit of capitalistic rage diluted by
cocktails in the musk of gold dinner lounges

He was slinking from jungle bush
to jungle bush
orange jessamine on the vine
I whispered a little prayer for him
after I rolled him back to nothing
even though I didn't go to church
and didn't know what to say
please I'm sorry I'm sorry—
my tongue was the pulpit
my teeth a long line of pews

And if you're asking me if I killed a queen
yes I did and I feel good about it
She was floating in a circular pool
spiked with goat's milk by her henchmen—
tits perfect, afloat—
gold necklaces flashing in the sunset of the
candlelight like the blade in my left fist

When the water turned red it filtered
out in little estuaries, ran warm fingers

through her hair—
men at the door like battering rams
and the live snake I brought
gliding toward her
toward the gold flakes of her pie-pan eyes
toward her mouth that was open
and drinking—
lactic acid, platelets, plasma

And I call this one Lusty Heretic
Floating Clockwise in a Sea of Her Own Blood
the snake swimming now inside her
deep down the stretching tunnel of her throat
a black bomb
She floats
and floats away
and dies out in the middle—
a rotation of dead stars

And the snake is back again
coiled around my arm
I'll put him back in the bushes
just where I found him
where his skin baked in that
grim summer asphalt
and feed him a clementine
a capful of cold water
and we'll talk about groves
as the sun grows low again

All Saints' Day
Philip Madden

A slate sky folds downward,
pressing the light into a thin seam—
a shadow untethered, hunting rest.

Air, stripped of scent, bears only the hint of
smoulder—
the ghosts of leaves burning,
an offering to what does not ask.

The breath carries frost,
promise of dawns scabbed with ice,
and the leaves—tiny firebrands—
flicker in spirals, scrawling elegies
on the cooling earth.

Above the treetops, wings wheel—
not many, not loud—
a pattern too precise for chance.

Darkness does not fall here; it accumulates—
a slow drowning in indigo.
The horizon fades to gauze,
a smudged border
where flame and time burn down to silence.

In the hush: a presence.
Not one, but many.
Their footfalls mimic the rustling canopy,
whispers borne on brittle stems.

A feather drifts—singed at the edge—
caught in the breathless dusk.

The world listens.
Sky holds its breath.
Time rotates—quiet, inevitable,
a slow wheel turning beneath veils.

And in the hush between wingbeats,
something is remembered.

Petals Severed
Shane David Morin

She plucks petals, "he loves me, he loves me not…"
Each petal a carmine artery unwound
From bone and cavity, each pluck a death,
her caresses strip, thorns dismembered,

these petals decayed, carmine artery wound
a tightrope walked once upon a time,
her caresses become thorns, dismembers
each appendage, severs muscle from sinew,

the tightrope taut once, this time
a final pluck, the stem left on table,
appendages severed, muscle & sinew
stripped away, my love the petal, cut.

A final pluck, stem tossed on table,
She plucked petals, says she loves me not,
Strips away my love, the petal cut
From bone & cavity, each pluck a death.

Sonnet Ouroboros
Shane David Morin

Love lies bloody, heart spurts like papercuts
Fingers crimsoned & crippled, reach for hand
Or face or simple embrace, falls to side
Like maple leaves, Autumn the harbinger
Of winter's death-grip. You stand as if to
Swing the axe, my body rigid splinters
Under a head dulled: I am not the first
Near miss of blade's kiss, splits insect wing,
A torso left six-legged, a flight risk
of urbanized massacres. And I crawl
semi-dismembered, my blood the breadcrumbs
left like children seeking the long road home.
This jagged journey becomes a slow death,
I awake & rise to see you once again.

I wake & rise to see you once again,
Wedding photos along the walls, askew
A few bent under the sheer weight of
Ravaged years, the centerpiece of younger "us"
A guillotine poised overhead, rope cut,
My head and pillory acquainted well
this final breath an "I love you," the thwack
becomes gift of head in wicker basket.
On opposing wall lies art framed sayings:
From this day forward, you are my only
Love and other tacky phrases which line
Living room walls, this sacred space becomes
Mausoleum, our memories exhume
Graves, silence the hammer, your hand, the nails.

Graves, silence the hammer, your hand, the nails
Claw at optic nerves, I gaze out window
Glazed with crimson frost, this winter wonder-
Land like Martian soil: chill & desolate.
You speak my name like a child, high and soft.
So I glance back, sapphire eyes become snare
As they did in '16: Portsmouth, first date:
Our first snowfall white as wedding dresses,
Imprinted on the grey matter, enshrined
As jesus' nails, bloody & rusted.
There's a wildfire on the horizon, I ask
Is that ash that falls confetti tonight?
You call my name as a warden, enchain
In panopticon prison. Always the Watcher.

In panopticon prison, always the Watcher
Sees without sight, hears without vocal echo,
Concrete walls & iron bars a refuge
(or so I'm told by voice & megaphone).
This cot & saturated mattress pad
Stained with piss & sweat & dried pools of blood,
Too tainted for even city rats or
The hissing cockroaches, my only friends.
Always the Watcher gazes from tower,
I pray to the great eye in the center,
Never knowing if or when she watches,
Surrender flesh & marrow, the altar
Laid bare as bone, this blood my sacrifice
To she who scrapes out rations of her love.

To she who scrapes out rations of her love:
Have you heard the cry of the lovesick dove?
His coo the sour chord struck, toothless pianos
Played by ex-lovers, one-handed, so it goes.

I too know why the caged dove cries, his tear
Slides down side of cheek, salinizes feather
Drops to cage foundation in a brief plop
Dissipates as quickly as it's made, a thought
Aphotic, these daily rations scattered
Like these tuxedo tails, serrated with
Razored nails, my skin left dripping crimson.
I would like to fly far from grasping claws,
This certificate fanged as a gaping maw.

This certificate fanged as a gaping maw,
Hung as heads on Vlad's pointed pikes
Framed like trophies upon this mildewed wall.
Slithering somewhere along the old fire-
Place, coral snake absently snacks on tail,
Black scales fade to red, teeth sink subdermal.
Still it slithers circular, still it flails
To release itself and let blood curdle.
I lie beside this ouroboral coral,
Curl to fetal, the members glow with revenge
These framed nuptials once believed immortal
Decay to desolation. We pretend
I'm Prince Charming, that we long abandoned "us,"
Love lies bloody, heart spurts like papercuts.

The Love of an Undead
Emrecan Doğan

Do you remember me;
You made fun of me like everyone else
With my broken glasses and my lame feet
And my other various flaws
Now I was;
With my shroud that fell from your shoulder
Now you have only me in your hands everywhere
I will do it;
The life of the mirror in your eyes without interruption
I will do it;
Among the shadows you see moving
I will do it;
In the crackling sounds when you are alone at home
You will never be able to escape;
Even if you are buried in your grave
One day in your sleep
It will slip from under your pillow
And press your face
Before you even understand what happened
I will take your breath away
I will fulfill my oath of revenge
I will take my revenge
And your soul
It will be all in return
For your love that you don't care about

the rope: the pinhole: the silhouette
Phillip Hurt

The black nothingness, overwhelming
Escape but a pinhole
Salvation from above, out of focus

"Help! I'm down here!" I yelled
I screamed it at the top of my lungs
    praying my cries would be heard

I almost can make out what once was out of focus
Closer I came, the pinhole, a silhouette within
A rope lowered, the offer of escape

"Please! Take the rope…
…I will help you"
The silhouette's words echoed

The rope, the help: well within my reach
The fibers, faint due to the callousness
Fingers worn, heart tender

A mere taste of the offering
Was it purposeful?
To not grasp what was sent from above

The silhouette, the rope: empty handed
"Why did you not accept?
The help sent forth?" bellowed the silhouette

Nothingness, like a weighted blanket
Comforting; Calming; Slowed pulse

"Leave me! I do not want your help!"

***

Blackness, now smothering
Stones, crushing my sternum
Course sand, filling my mouth

"Please! Take the rope…
…I will help you!"
The silhouette's words desperately echo

--the rope--
    tendons anchor the filaments
    the void giving it life

--the pinhole--
    infinite in structure
    possibilities from what's beyond

--the silhouette--
    the darkest shadow, familiar
    fierce vibrations above

I shed the obstructions
As I free the boulder and coarse sand
"I will accept your help," now but a whisper

Fingers circumference the rope
    morph into a noose with ease
The fallen crown takes its place at my collar

As the ground gains in distance
No hesitation or panic

Blackness reversed

The pinhole enlarging as I approach
The silhouette, no longer a haze
Recognizing myself, as I take my last breath

The Weatherworker's Wife
Anna Remennik

Authors note: These poems are written in the style of Russian romance songs, where action is frequently revealed through dialogue, but in a setting where magic and magical transformation are possible. Because a lot of each poem is dialogue, the different speakers are distinguished via italic or bold text

The fell winds howl outside,
Like beasts in pain or fear,
Behind the door – a haven safe,
With flame and warmth and cheer.

"Why have you shorn your tresses, love?
What dread news fills your ear?
Whom has blind, ruthless fate struck down,
Among those you hold dear?

Is it your mother or your sire,
Is it your sister fair,
On whose account you've donned the grey
And shorn your lovely hair?"

"My mother's well as well can be,
My father keeps from harm,
My sister fair has given me
No reason for alarm.

Sad, sudden news have reached my ear,
And reached it all too slow:
Sad news that your apprentice-Mage
Has perished in the snow.

He rode out on a sunny day,
His staff across the bow,
He rode out on a sunny day,
And perished in the snow."

"Oh, winter is a wicked foe,
And he was but half-taught.
A pity that he should be lost,
And all my work for naught."

"The blizzard struck from clear skies
When snow began to fall,
The winds rose up so sudden-stark,
As to a master's call."

"Oh, winter is a wicked foe,
And she will have her play.
A rare Mage could call such storms
Out of a cloudless day."

"He rode out on a sunny day,
Upon a sunlit rise,
But stealthy fog wrapped him in dark
And muffled all his cries.

The winter winds rose up to wail
And rend with icy claws,
They tore the forked staff from his hands
And from his back his clothes.

His mare ran headlong through the murk,
Slashed by the winds so keen;
Now ice lay slick beneath her hooves
Where sound earth had been.

They both cried out then, man and horse,
And screaming, thrashing, fell—"
"Where have you heard this tale, my love,
Which you recount so well?"

"He lay upon the icy bank,
With snow falling fast,
Maimed horse beside, no man behind,
And knew this day his last.

He may have been but poorly taught,
But his own gift was rich,
And death and love, they taught him then
What no Mage him would teach.

He called the snow, he called the wind,
And gave them shape and name,
And gave it four ice-crystal hooves
And snow-white tail and mane.

He gave it voice in singing ice,
Pure as a silver bell,
He gave it breath in winter wind,
And gave his tale to tell.

The storm-steed ran through howling winds,
Through swirling snow and gloom,
Its crystal hooves struck stars from ice,
Made lakes with hoarfrost bloom.

It breathed upon my window pane
And touched it with its horn –
I knew at once what news it bore

And wherefore came this storm.

"The man who steps on new-formed ice
Has but himself to blame;
The man who loves another's wife,
He starts a deadly game.

A rare Mage may call such storms
Out of a cloudless sky.
But for the sake of my wife's love
So rare a Mage am I."

She cried out like a wounded bird
At what she'd guessed before,
She left her sleeve clutched in his hand
And wrestled past the door.

She flew into the raging storm
To meet her love once more –
And where a grey-gowned girl had run
A white dove rose to soar.

The storm died quick as it had come,
Restoring cloudless skies;
They found a dead man by his horse,
Tears frozen in his eyes.

As if by scores of vicious knives
His bloodied clothes were torn.
They found his forked staff far behind,
Among the thicket thorns.

And, in a sight none could explain,
As if returned to nest,
There lay a lifeless, frozen bird,
A white dove, on his breast.

As they had found them, man and bird,
So they were laid to rest –
The Weatherworker with his staff
The white dove on his breast.

The Apple Tree
Anna Remennik

"You are the flower of my spring!"
(by root and branch and twisting vine)
"You are the fruit of everything!"
(the flower blooms in its own time.)

"Now I am going far from home."
(by root and branch and twisting vine)
"And I shall be left all alone."
(the flower blooms in its own time.)

"To you I shall be always true,"
(by root and branch and twisting vine)
"Then I shall stay and wait for you."
(the flower blooms in its own time.)

"The nights are dark, the days are long…"
(by root and branch and twisting vine)
"But I shall wait and fear no wrong…"
(the flower blooms in its own time.)

"I spoke these words so long ago…"
(by root and branch and twisting vine)
"But I shall trust until I know…"
(the flower blooms in its own time.)

"It was a foolish vow of youth…"
(by root and branch and twisting vine)
"But I shall wait to hear the truth…"
(the flower blooms in its own time.)

"Once we were both so young and fair…"
(by root and branch and twisting vine)
"Though I have waited past my share…"
(the flower blooms in its own time.)

"I've met another just as dear…"
(by root and branch and twisting vine)
"Such a long time I've lingered here…"
(the flower blooms in its own time.)

"Long since forgotten there, I swear!"
(by root and branch and twisting vine)
"I've waited all my heart could bear."
(the flower blooms in its own time.)

"I'm free to love and free to wed thee!"
(by root and branch and twisting vine)
"I vowed never to forget thee…"
(the flower blooms in its own time.)

"Our love will be our greatest good."
(by root and branch and twisting vine)
"My heart will turn to silent wood…"
(the flower blooms in its own time.)

"Our love is strong beyond belief."
(by root and branch and twisting vine)
"My words will turn to rustling leaves…"
(the flower blooms in its own time.)

"Our love will never disappear."
(by root and branch and twisting vine)
"My grief will turn to tree-sap clear…"
(the flower blooms in its own time.)

"My heart is broken and betrayed…"
(by root and branch and twisting vine)
"My human thoughts and memories fade…"
(the flower blooms in its own time.)

"I shall return where my love waits."
(by root and branch and twisting vine)
"If you come now, you come too late…"
(the flower blooms in its own time.)

"Where is the one who waited true?"
(by root and branch and twisting vine)
– This apple-tree now waits for you.
(the flower blooms in its own time.)

"Its crown murmurs up above,"
(by root and branch and twisting vine)
"Its branches blossom with our love."
(the flower blooms in its own time.)

"A golden apple, ripe and bright"
(by root and branch and twisting vine)
"It bears all for my delight"
(the flower blooms in its own time.)

"Such faithful love's a shame to waste,"
(by root and branch and twisting vine)
"This fruit will bear its gentle taste,"
(the flower blooms in its own time.)

"This fruit, the essence of her soul…"
(by root and branch and twisting vine)
"But it is bitter, bile and gall,"

(the flower blooms in its own time.)

"It stings my throat, it burns like lye!"
(by root and branch and twisting vine)
"I fear I'm lost... I know I die…"
(the flower blooms in its own time.)

By root and branch and twisting vine
The flower blooms in its own time.

H o t e l of   L o n g i n g
Jennifer Londry

Two thugs outside of a hotel on a dead-end street,
stand beside two empty flowerpots that smell
like Columbian coffee.
The men's faces are pock-marked and rubbery with big
blabby lips.
Sign above the door says, Rooms to Let.
She enters and takes the pocket-sized elevator up the
six-foot incline, she needs to turn sideways, walk
crablike, to inch her way inside.
Strange arrival.
Victorian   Empress   chandelier   illuminates   the
reception desk,   vacant.
There is only room for three incoming,   and   one
outgoing guest.
She sits.
She knows to rush, is to miss the journey.
Locals refer to the place as, the *Hotel of Longing*.
Pictures of faceless queens line the walls.
Rugs from Turkey absorb the cool of the marble tiled
floor.
Out an open window four funerary carollers, whistling
a dirge,
just as a dove flies in the window, gets tangled in the
flotilla
of hanging crystals.
Purple light flashes.
Barcode required.
Swallow.

She climbs a flight of stairs no wider than a palm print.

Unit No. 4.
Reserved for
new arrivals. The shrunken. The ill. The sick and
tired of gone glory.
One-room suite with keyless entry.
No bed
No key
On an invisible nightstand,
a sad little fishbowl sits empty.

At the bottom of a red velvet escalator.
Unit No. 3
A well appointment room with a threadbare two-
legged ottoman, and
a chatty green sofa.
A cup of Espresso.
The Ohm of spiritual discomfort.
A two-burner hotplate serves as a stove, but there's
no power.
Electricity can be purchased at the entrance to the
hotel,
at a cost of three dollars per day.
Nickel-eye-slot jiggety wires.
Yak Yak Yak telephone talks to itself.

Up a spiral staircase made from bloodwood. A
blue door.
Unit No. 2
It's a little more reserved.
Less communicative.
Big screen television is a yawn. Gap between
its teeth a

> bullet hole.
> She steps into the void.
> Express Dumb waiter.

Unit No. 1
Opulent.
Antique mercury glass mirrored ceiling.
Candelas in the hands of naked stone statues.
Curvy champagne flutes.
White satin sheets.
A bed of nails made of diamonds.

> A unique feature of the room is the dial-up
> wallpaper.
> Snow covered birch trees dotted with red
> robins.
> Fresh fields of marmalade-coloured tulips
> popping out of ditches
> along a highway.
> Desert sun, hot skin peel. Rain on toast.

[] [] [][] [ ] [ ] [ ] [ ] [ ][][][][][]

Assembly of wooden deck chairs
on a floating dock that faces towards a portrait
of a blue freshwater   lake.

[] [] [][] [ ] [ ] [ ] [ ] [ ][][][][][]

Yonder, a stroll in the orchard
to observe the workers that toil on ladders built slender
at the top.
Or wait out the seasons,   watch   the pickers' fall
like rotten apples   cracked   /   heads   leaking
pesticides.

[] [] [][] [ ] [ ] [ ] [ ][][][][][]

A group of well-dressed scarecrows
sit on stumps perched too close to a
bonfire, backs turned.
SHIVER

[] [] [][] [ ] [ ] [ ] [ ][][][][][]

Turnstile.
Circus tents
one-legged clowns juggling
chainsaws. Candyfloss maker looks on in
amusement, stirs the pink.

Ferris-wheel of first love.
Sky high. Wobbly joyride, fear, excitement, two
heads knock good sense into one another.
When the hotel lights start to flicker. It is time for
guest number one to leave.
Trap door opens. Jackassery tumble
into cock-a-hoop.

My Heart
Richard Simonds

after Stephen Crane

My heart is very large,
Come and join the bloody feast,
You who held me tight last night,
Pressed hard against your body,
I love you and so many others,
But you cannot have it all,
Others are greedily
Gorging on what they can,
And there are bitter parts
That are not so tasty,
And the hidden dark parts
No one can ever reach,
No matter how deep
The cut with the knife.

My heart beats quickly
When I think of you,
When I press against you,
You can feel the deep rich
Blood pulse, the red surge
Pumped through my body,
So much life-energy here,
Bursting within me,
So much to share.

My heart craves to be devoured
By the starving and desperate,
Touch me and feel it,

All I have to give
Is in the present moment,
There is no future with me,
The past is long forgotten,
I am the best of lovers,
If love is all you want,
If you want to taste desire,
        and feed, feed, feed.

Who Loved Her

Veronica Kegel-Giglio

I am the warlock of Whitfield
who fell in love with a beautiful maiden

I saw her, and she stole my heart,
and so I watched her from afar

Then I started writing her letters
pledging my love for her

She wrote back pledging her love for me
stating we were destined to be forever

Our correspondence was full of love and commitment,
but I was worried

What would she think about my practice of the dark arts
and my ugly face

But she sounded intrigued by my witchcraft
and was eager to meet

I did not tell her about my warts,
discolored skin, and deformed face

We agreed to meet by the light of the moon
near a quiet old bridge

When she saw me,
she screamed and cried

Then she ran away from me
and stumbled at the bridge's edge

She fell into the water
head first and drowned

Now I am alone
and without love or hope

Because I Saw You
Alexander Marais

We were walking down the street, in a manner I would have liked to think entailed us holding hands. But that, of course, is where the imaginary aspect must come into play.

She was skipping down the street, though. I don't have to edit that into my memory.

Every now and then, she would turn and look back at me - a semi-trusting half-smile on her face. "Is it close?" she would ask.

She would ask that more than once...

I would always smile, and nod my head. "Over there, only just."

She was so beautiful. Her long locks of blonde hair almost wafting across her shoulders, her face a portrait of developed innocence. I wish I had a picture of her in the moment. The aforementioned traits were so stunning, juxtaposed against the rustling wind, the bright green leaves on either side - some detached and dancing across the pavement. The environment extending itself to the point of being so wide, so open. So perfect, really.

Have you ever thought of a moment in time, sublime enough you'd live in it forever? That was me, in that moment. Following Alicia down to the coast, on a beautiful summer day on Old County Road, in York, Maine. It was August of 1992. Oddly enough the ensuing feelings leave an almost bitter taste in my mouth. Particularly in the rare occasions I visit that place. I stand by the water, and let the tips of the small waves massage my toes.

Cape Neddick Park always is beautiful, even during a slight, Autumn chill. Feelings don't come easily to me, you see. There's an almost arduous process of bringing out a specific emotion, a sort of dance and ritual I do to myself. Mercifully, just the biting nature of the corners of water embedding themselves beneath cuticles can coax. If only just.

"Why are we here?"

The words dance through my head, time and again. I smile every time at the memory. Then the full-on acuity fades, and I start to forget. That climax makes me feel sad. I start to forget every dimension of her face. In some ways, it helps me fill in the blanks with what I would like to remember. In other ways, such implementations are just all around dispiriting. Nothing really goes perfectly in life, one's fantasy alternates not always aligning either.

I look down at my toes again, and blink back the tears in my eyes. Her question, for whatever reason, is always last to fade.

Why are we here?

"Because I saw you," I hear myself say, repeating what was said all those years ago. "Because I saw you…"

Dear Y
Kad the Poet

A thousand years ago
You said to me
Only you could be the sole carrier
Of the burden I exist as
That no other soul could come close
I just want to inform you
In the end
It was not I
Who was the burden

Not OK
Kad the Poet

How are you?
I don't know
My love is gone
And a piece of me with them
The sun went out
My sky is now bleak
Leaving me surrounded
By thick darkness
My soul carries
The weight of them
My heart will never be the same
So please be gentle
As I try to learn
How to live this life
Without the best thing that was in it

Soldier
Kad the Poet

I would burn
For a thousand days

I would take
Your blame and pain

I would endure
The swords and spears

I would bear the arrows
And the knives in my back

I suffered everyday
For you

But you would never
Take a scratch for me

Someday
Kad the Poet

All I have is a promise
A "we will, someday"
I want to believe
To hope and dream
And keep holding on
But there it is
"Tomorrow"
"Next week"
"Next month"
"Next year"
All I have is a promise
Change the calendar on the wall
Count the moons
The seasons cycle through
All I have is a promise
When what I wanted was
You

Unrequited Death
J Louis Messina

The day death claimed me,
Alone, eternally, I roam the Earth,
Seeking a lover,
My death like a birth.

Haunting your nightmares,
I whisper my name.
For you to accept me,
But you blow out my flame.

Your heart and soul
Belongs to another.
My rage for you
I need to smother!

You run from me
In darkened halls,
Screaming "help!"
Through hallowed walls.

Although you live,
And I am death.
Soon, my dearest, soon,
I snatch your breath.

As bloody you perish
In lover's arms.
Your soul drifts to me
In sanguine alarms.

At last! In afterlife I own you,
A ghostly journey with mine.
"Damn you!" for your paramour
You do pine.

Whilst you prowl his fevered dreams,
He cries awake for you to feel.
My hunger, my lust for you
He does steal.

Your lover slit's his wrists,
For living and phantom to unite.
Though I stand in your way,
You both take flight!

Once more, I roam the Earth
As lovers spirit away.
For slaying you,
Alone, eternally, I must stay.

Gutted; Scarred; Heal
an ode to
the transforming power of horror
John Schlimm

ball of ground glass
            c h u r n *ssssss* in my groin
nicking rectum, drawing blackened   bloodied stool,
       s
      e
      s
     i
    it r . . . . slowly at first;

    tearing now through coiled intestines, uninhibited, pure evil
           s
            e
             s
             i
    ground glass ball r. . . . . fasterNOW,
    its shards of j
         a
         g
         g
           e
              d, uneven, ravenous devil teeth
   stab, chew, saw, rip kidneys bowels colon pancreas, bile
seeping,
   then it pauses in stomach to churn, to taunt, to nauseate,
   to wrench gut   until it   bur n n n n
n*ssss*;

i

ground glass ball . . . . . r i s e s . . . . . fasterNOW,
puncturing, busting, exploding into
solar plexus, thensettlingin;   *s*

       s

      s

     t

    o

    o

   h

every nerve ending s   brainward,
like long, gnarled, sizzling fingernails
s l a s hing / d i gging into three-pound organ, eviscerating,
  p u ll i n g slimy strings of matter from broken
skull,
 leaving them—like dying worms—strewn, wriggling,
splattered
       e
on floor and c r   c k l d stre e t ;
    a

ground glass ball twists round and round,
teasing fasterFASTER, intense, then moreINTENSE,
teasing until body is an inferno:

     flames
        flicking, licking
      spewing
    s h ards, slive r s
   c h u nks of p a i n, debris
  slit t ing , minc ing their cruel w a y
through b o d y m i n d s p i r i t, no mercy, no relief
"SOMEONE, ANYONE, P L E A S E HELP
MEEEEEEEEEEE,"
 i scream; i screamISCREAM;
      but I do not stop I do not stop will not
stop do not end
 ;

the horror

no . . .

ahhhhhhhhhhhhhhhhhhhhhhhhhhhh, THE HORROR—

written, spoken, sung, filmed, performed, drawn,
dr p i n   from blades, s c r aaa t c h e d into splintered wood,
   i p   g
a n y medium—
channel it, process it, create it:

Michael, Jason, Freddy,
                Art, Jigsaw,
                        Chucky, Candyman, Ghostface,
                                        Hannibal,
                                Leatherface,

                    M3GAN

                                            Nor
                                            man,
God's Satan, my own Viper;

        horror: you   breathe   air   into   our
        souls;
    help us face our darkest fears, confront our torture, stare down
demons eating us inside out;

    oh, THE HORROR . . .
    dear horror:

you transform the voracious, bloodied, gut-wrenching ball of
ground glass
into creative juices, finely-minced and blended, then boiled
into power—
our darkness, our scars, finally recognized and spoken aloud—
you, HORROR, you empower
me

to

heal . . .

Viewing Room
Nina Poe

The room is dark and plain.
His face is drawn and gray.

Outside, the day is warm and bright.
In the sun, there's grass
and roses and a little
dog who barks.

In the room,
there's a gray couch
with a stain.
Orchids that aren't quite
White.

His eyes are closed,
his mouth is poised
with wire and a string.
There are chemicals inside him,
I want to touch his hand, but
I can't quite
can't quite
Look
at him.

Some say the dead smell,
but there is no smell in here.
The room is quiet and cool,
an air conditioner hums
somewhere behind my head.

His head is quiet now,
there is no endless humming.
(Unlike mine.)
I wish

I could curl up on this couch
and sleep for a few hours,
maybe five.

And they
could wheel me in
where he was
and fix me –

Quiet the brain,
Close the eyes,
Sew up the lips
into a peaceful smile.

Ghost Lover
Nina Poe

I couldn't sleep again last night. So, you didn't come to me, hanging there glorious like silver slippers dangling from the rafters. I had to close my eyes to picture you and then you were dancing around the periphery. Never sitting there with your sunglasses on, the light filtering through some dead, nearby tree. Shadows across your lovely face: a dark room full of smoke, living room filled with grass. I wish you would come to me again. Never in your body, but only in dreams. That's when you're most lovely.

Holding my hand, tracing your fingers through my guts. Bloody cuticles all churning through me. I'd lick each finger. And I know it's wrong to want the things I want: to want the hollow eyes and the way you tilt when you look away from me. I know it's wrong to want you for who you no longer are. But you're lovely in my dreams. Telling me it's okay. Pulling me out. Giving me a reason.

Even if you're never mine in day-time, I'll always have you. Always turn beneath those eyes: mahogany brown delicious like a new life on satin pillows, the earth reeking beneath. I can see the clouds in the sky: torn cotton hinting at heaven. Thank you for even the hardest days. Because I know, afterward, I'll find you there, hovering above the pillow.

Cannibalism
Espi Kvlt

Eat of my body,
I sacrifice it to you.
On the altar of lust,
plants from my bones grew.

The darkness swept in
to this cave we call home
and from its blanketed branches
our life collapsed like Rome.

And from its death
new existence sprang forth
and piled upon the shadows
like snow in the north.

Now I lie here in wait
for your teeth in my flesh
and I crave the cold feeling
of your satisfied thresh.

My lungs become dust
and my heart becomes air
and my blood becomes yours
and my hair becomes theirs.

Anastasis
Espi Kvlt

I fall through rose petals
with your blood on my lips.
I dance in the dark
with the moon on my skin.
I lie in the dirt
and whisper your name.
I long for the touch
of your teeth in my veins.

I scrape off my skin
in piles for your collection.
I rip out my heart
with scalpels for your dissection.
I sleep in a coffin
and cry out our song.
I beg you for mercy
as loud as the night is long.

Your tongue is like knives
as it laps at my throat.
Your words are like poison
as they tranquilize me slow.
I die in this prison
you built out of thorns.
I thank you for helping me –
I am reborn.

I Hope I Haunt You
Espi Kvlt

I am the ghost in your bedroom
that creaks against your floorboards
when you're certain you're alone.
I am whispering into your ear
reminding you what you did to me
and telling you what I'll do to you.
You will never again know a night of peace,
for you took all of mine and buried it
all the way down into your gut
beneath the mud and the grime.
My rain will pour down inside of you
and bury it deeper
until it mixes into the walls of your organs
and all my pain and all my rage
will become one with your body.
I am the spectre that inhabits your bones.
This isn't a dream, nor a nightmare;
this is the reality you left me with.
This is the reality I leave you with.

He Tasted So Good
Veronica Kegel-Giglio

I fell in love with him at the beach after we swam in
the sea together
We made love on a blanket under the moon, and he
said he loved my poetry and my face
We made promises to each other, and we vowed to
love each other forever
Then one day he told me he had met another to love,
and he would not disclose the person's gender
I was so mad, I flew into a rage, and I killed him with
my father's service revolver
I cut off his head, and I cooked his brains
They tasted so good
And then I hacked up the rest of his body and organs,
and I ate them
He did taste good.

The Knots in the Wood
Tinamarie Cox

I bought this package of matches to burn it all down.

I will watch
  the flames start small
  and grow,
as the fire devours all the rot my love has become.

It should feel like a terrible crime
  to rob my mind of the delusion.
Ignorance had been a numbing bliss.
Knowledge gutted me
   with the unlocked Pandora's box.
All the secrets falling out in the open,
  and yet,
  not seen through my eyes.

Our defects were camouflaged as smiles in the knots
  in the wood.
Wood that I will set ablaze with just a tiny match.

I Loved Him Until My Death
Veronica Kegel-Giglio

I cannot describe how great my love for him was, but he rocked my world at that dance

We danced always and made love under the moonlight with passion and kink

He bought me perfume and trinkets, and we had lavish picnic feasts

I could never picture life without him

He vowed to marry me the night I told him I was pregnant, and I slept sweetly after he proposed

I dreamed about our wedding and the family we would make together

But he smothered me as I slept killing me and our unborn child because he wanted another

He found another prettier and younger lady, and I have vowed. revenge

I haunt them every night bellowing and screaming

I will drive them to insanity or death whichever comes first

Killing me was a BIG mistake

To a Jealous Lowlife
A.J. Chilson

Ever since you felt the need to start shit,
My mission has been to let you have it.

For all the garbage I was made to take,
I just want to return that for my sake.

Not one time did I intend to cause strife,
As I've never wanted to fuck your wife.

Yet in a rage of unjust jealousy,
That is how you have made it out to be.

And it appears your anger will not cease,
Now that you've threatened to call the police.

That goes to illustrate how very low
A person you are, who deserves a throw.

Yes, I would love to knock you to the ground,
Because I'll never let you put me down.

I'm a much better person than you think,
And rest assured, I'll make your ego sink.

You won't get by with being an asshole;
No, you'll be like a bean bag in cornhole.

Then, when you've finally learned your lesson,
There will be changes made to your person.

Mental Illness
A.J. Chilson

I don't know what made me want to do this,
Or how I thought it would be glamorous.

While on my break, I was feeling down,
Wondering just why I'm even around.

Back on the clock, I was sweeping the lot;
A cigarette butt appeared on the spot.

It was my job to place it in the trash;
To that, I did – after I got a rash.

That's because, if only on a bad day,
I made my arm out to be an ashtray.

All I can say is, I wasn't thinking,
As self-destruction was in the making.

Friends, when mental illness happens to you,
You do things you normally wouldn't do.

As a result, there are consequences,
And you will be coming to your senses.

For me, all I ever got was a scar
On my arm; that told me I went too far.

The fact that I still work is a blessing;
Otherwise, life could be more distressing.

Inheritance
J. J. Munro

Shadows, always shadows,
not on the path, in his mind.
Branches ache in the wood's
close quarters, old trees weep,
moon-clustered clouds
join the conspiracy. He lurches
through the iron gates, eyes set
on the big house, slumbering, still.
His house, once!
Key in one hand, knife in the other,
he has long planned this bloodbath,
snatches of memory taunting him
in his lonely cell, memories of his wife
and his brother who abandoned him,
sent him to the asylum, stealing his
rightful inheritance.
Tonight, he escaped and
they would now inherit —
his revenge.

Vanished
John Kujawski

I had hoped that someday she'd simply reappear
She's the one who helped me with all my deep and inner
fear
My deep anxieties no longer brought me any pain
The first thing she did was show me the open flame

I had a fear of fire and stayed away from smoke
She'd look at me and laugh like it was all a joke
She'd burn things in front of me like a clever arsonist
She had the hottest temper ever and one I couldn't resist

She destroyed everything that was ever in her path
She was a stunning goth girl turning conflict into craft
When fire no longer scared me she planned her clever
little attack
She made me have an addiction but it wasn't heroin or
crack

She went after me with obsession until I finally responded
My social anxiety was erased and soon we were truly
bonded
American Top 40 was suddenly kicked straight to the
curb
She replaced it with Peter Murphy and then The
Psychedelic Furs

She was a stunning angel who was pale and dressed in
black
Then one day she was gone and I never got her back
I was told sometimes people vanish or simply go away

Their souls don't even care if you kneel down and you pray

Sometimes I check the graveyards to see if she has a stone.
I hope she'll come back a zombie and then I won't be left alone
For her I'd light a candle or set a bunch fields on fire
She's destroyed my phobias but replaced them with desire

All I Hear is You
Juan Ozuna

Look at the night sky,
an infinity of stars,
that don't match your eyes.

"Where's everyone at?"
"They're gone."
she points up
at little human shapes
getting smaller and smaller
struggling
so many bodies
they block the stars and turn the sky into a black ceiling
"Now there's no stars to compare me to."

Your smile sends waves of
dopamine, you're like a sea
and I am drowning.

"That's not rain…is it?"
a sticky shower
upon my face and chest and eyes
congealing thick and tasting metal
she and i look like newborns
ripped from a mother's womb
so much blood covering my skin
i might be inside out
a heart plops in front of me

from those people in the sky
up there is a movement
a pulsing like waves
as if the sky is an ocean
"I'll give you a sea."
her face hardens into corners
and blood pours faster
showers – drenches everything
everywhere a landscape of crimson
thick red puddling, now pooling
now rivers and streams
she's twisting their bodies
way up there
wringing them like towels
intestines catch on power lines
limbs flop like fallen birds
heads rain down and beat the ground, now a rising sea
and i am swept away in it all
drowning in viscera and neural matter
swallowed into a maelstrom of broken hearts
until she pulls me out

I have been waiting
for you to take your last breath.
Till then, time goes slow.

she reads my poem
then runs outside
sinking to her shins
in a mixture of blood
and bone and dermis
then turns back to me
with a smile that trembles

"I wish your heart bursts!"
and once this wish is voiced
it comes true, like all the rest
like wishing people to float up
she explodes
spreads herself everywhere
like stardust in an expanding universe
she destroyed everything in my life
broke pieces off me
and left me misshapen
yet I still loved her
was still grateful to wake up
next to her
i wish i could take back what I wrote
but she is dead now
so i lay down
covering myself in her
i'm sinking in human remnants
chunks getting in my mouth
my eyes, my ears
blocking all sound and sight
there's a buzzing like galaxies crashing
as i die it is like…

I am listening
to a universe screaming
her name everywhere.

This Mortal Coil
Mark Alan Furini

I hate this heart,
This mortal coil.
This broken, battered,
Torn up heart.
This heart that bleeds
And beats for you.
This heart that pumps
And flows and spews.
It thrums and melts
And traps me there
With you.
I hate this heart
This mortal coil.
This busted, shattered,
Ripped up heart.
This heart that beats
And bleeds for you.
It thumps and breaks
And haunts me there
With you.
I hate this heart,
This mortal coil.
This broken, battered,
Torn up heart.
This heart that bleeds
And beats for you.
At last...it stops.
And ends with you.

Come To Me
Ian Klink

Come to me, as I open my body to the frigid night
Come to me for when I last saw you, embraced in fright
Come to me as I look upon the blood-red moon
Come to me, as I shiver with lust, quite rightly soon

Could you hate me with all the love of your heart?
Could you hate me when I try to stop what you start?
Could you hate me when my rage uncontrollably spins?
Could you hate me as I open my breast to all these
hearty sins?

I had never seen a face with such longing and fear
As if you wanted everyone in eternity to clear
Your face was aghast from the centuries of punishment
Please embrace my love with wonder and astonishment

Could you still love me when you know what I know?
Could you still love me with all your hate in tow?
Could you still love me when you did the deed you
tried?
Could I still love you with the deed I helped hide?

You have lived the lives of many men, their blood flows
through your veins
With each bite, you conquer their worries and unlock
their mortal chains
My wish to be lost in the castle of your eternally dying
chamber

If you only knew the power you hold over my infatuated
soul, a flaming ember

Could you look past the blood on my hand?
Could you look past the time we had?
Could you look past the hatred and smell?
Could you look past my deathly spell?

What was it that changed you into this?
A killer of innocent lives, with just a sharp pointed kiss?
As I lay in the dirt, awaiting your sweet voice and
alluring breath
How could my prince be the welcome of such hideous
death?

Could you judge me for how much I care?
Could you judge me for my grim stare?
Could you judge the blade in my palm?
Could you blame me for how I never stayed calm?

It seems so odd you would spare my life, as I stumbled
upon the moonlit garden
Shaking from the chilly air, my entire body already
hardened
Then I saw the eyes, which beamed darkened red
My heart pounded with such fiery rage and dread

Would your eyes pierce through the blackness inside?
Could you forgive me if I strode our love in stride?
Would you take me in your arms, hot and sweaty, with
haste?
Could you possibly see me through the bloody mess,
post haste?

Yet it was then that relief overcame my existence,
propelling my calm
My fingers relaxed as my nails pierced the flesh of my
palm
Would this sinner, ripping the skin of its victim's nape
Metamorphosis into a saint, letting me step back, a
narrow escape

Is this the end of our love that starts?
Two broken lovers, with shattered hearts?
Is there an end to the dessert of your soul
Or an ocean of feelings so deep in a hole?

It dropped its meal upon the mud, a splash of earth upon
its feet
The eyes seemed to expand their glow, a masterful trick
of a magician's feat
Then it leaped into the crystal-clear sky without even a
slight sound
Leaving behind a victim in its hateful wake and
herculean bound

Are you the shadow that dances at night?
Will you spare me, not the dread of the fright?
Can you be so cold your eyes are black as ice?
Oh, please be my lover. Oh, please would not that be
nice?

I froze, as many would, not sure what to do in such a
wild fate
My thoughts speeding at a thousand miles a minute in a
cuckooed state

I searched around before tripping over the mess of your
victim
A scream alarming all who heard, making me the
propter delictum

What is I leave you, forever to search for me when I left
thee behind?
Would you follow me through time, the sands in the
wind leaving you blind?
Would you forget me like the dew on the morning
grass?
Could you cease searching, your morbid queen a
memory dying to pass?

Your eyes made me shiver with a passion for old
My body was on fire even in the winter's cold
You are the devil, a demon, a killer, above all
Yet I wait for you in darkness, heading your call

As I pick a flower off the grave, Can I leave this world I
love so dear?
Must my love for you be so venially clear?
Will you take me away, wrap my sorrow in a dark silky
veil
Could you find it in your heart to love forever, with no
avail?

As I wait by the graveside for my master to return
I feel the blood of your victim rolling to my feet, their
soul burn
I can see its body start moving, something inside its
shell strive
It reaches for my throat, its sensational appetite alive

Why was it not you, whom my beating heart I first
welcomed in?
Why could it not be you who takes the breath of my sin?
Why is it not you who looks into my eyes for
understanding?
Why not you who makes me know after I am dead with
you, I will be standing?

It loves me, yes. It loves not. It loves me, yes, it loves
not
Our love in death will not be for naught
It calls for me now, as it called for me then.
Its sharp teeth on my neck, my life for you, soon to end.

UNHOLY SEDUCTION
Jarrod Camiré

I can feel her, body, mind, and soul…

Her heart, so alive, governing this endless beating;

Exquisite countess, as of now, your existence and world keep on dancing…

Yet I'm getting closer, unreal, unseen;

Listening to your pulse, contemplating,

That red flow in your veins, which is so strong, so keen…

Such a color, that scarlet appears, this purest crimson,

Far truer whenever compared to that of an ephemeral rose;

Beware noble dame for as of now my hunger arose…

Know lady that I am already a lost soul, depraved, beyond redemption.

Thus, I am ready to seduce you, enthrall you; wholeheartedly I shall devour you…

And I have chosen the simplest of solutions, the most elaborate of deception.

Take heed fragile queen, for I am the fangs of the night.

I am only base longing, corruption, appetite;

Stronger than any mortal, I am nothing but intention, sheer might.

Now, do you feel it all around you? This crown of duplicity, this iron touch;

My bare embrace takes indeed the form of a cold, merciless clutch.

My accursed body and yours are lying down, quietly they intertwined...

Unholy desires in such ways before being created,

But tomorrow you won't remember such fleeting a moment.

Already only a faint impression remains; that, and your flesh, sore and elated.

Erotic sensations and so brief this common madness,

Our skin, a tender dream of forbidden pleasures;

Only abandon exists, profane sweetness…

My lips pressed at your so delicate neck,

Ivory shape, carnally those canines which pierce you,

Your entire self remains underneath me, shivering,
tantamount to a mere wreck…

And the dark finds you utterly lost, sad, and lonely,

While the morning is born anew in a single incandescent
ray;

Like me, will you also learn to hate the day?

Already you seek my nefarious shadow,

Your immaculate beauty shrouded by fragments of that
defunct night.

In that moment of revelation, thinking about us, do you
disavow?

Here and now, have you fathomed out your fate?

For you are long past midnight, darling, abandoned and
so affright;

Don't be, sweet love, even as die both your spirit and the surrounding light...

For in darkness, there exists a wonderful secret.

Hear the appalling truth, dear inamorata...

By our shared perversion, our souls altogether, utterly forfeit...

From today onward you'll be mine; evermore I'll be yours,

Unique shall be our damnation, eternal essences coalescing in a common sanctuary;

And in this lost palace I see us drinking blood evermore, for genuine is the wine of
Eternity...

God Carves the Dead, Too
James Patrick Riser

Her smile.
That's what got me.

She's always been made with
Delicate wrists and limbs like
Everything carved from fine
Caramel wood, smooth and
No knots. Brown eyes, deep pools.
Clearly
An uncaring God, staring
From a stoic, gray sky is
A master at its craft of creation.
Of destruction.

Sometimes, I suppose we must be
Reminded, reprimanded.

She still lives, my love
But the fine wood has turned sky gray
And dry, the pools in her face
Clouded like ash.
Film covered.
Mechanically rotating
Orbs in deep, black sockets.
They follow me throughout the room
They always have.
The sharp sound of skin peeling from bone,
Like the sound of tape pulled from wrapping paper,
And the anticipation of a gift.
She no longer has lips,

She smiles forever.

Romantic dinners.
Anniversaries, valentines and birthdays.
I still give her cards, and put them solemnly
On a dining table, bitten by age, rotten
By the pent up moister of
Pregnant clouds.
She is hand cuffed to the chair.
Metal eating into knotted wood.
Everything splinters more and more each year.
She hooks her hands, trying to reach into my chest.

She has my heart.
I imagine what it would look like if
She bit into the organ like a
Hallow shape of chocolate wrapped in
Crimson foil. Viscera dripping down her arm and
On the table with a wet smack.
Like a wet hand on a shower door,
Pulsating silhouettes of sex
Play on the back of my eyelids
when I can sleep.

The clacking of her teeth
A bare twitching nerve with black, peeling fingernails.

I'll always have her smile, and
When the wood finally snaps like
Like her exposed, yellowing bone,
She can have me, too.

Pretty Sins
Xtina Marie

a doll
with dark thoughts,
my sins
were pretty
and took
what they wanted,
what I needed

Intricate Blue Ribbons
Xtina Marie

there are times
late at night,
while I am lying
in bed
that I hear
the sound of the
wallpaper peeling--
small sections
of pale yellow
surrounding
intricate blue ribbons
flaking off
to collect in a pile
on the dusty floor

but when I check
the next morning
I am always
shocked
to see the baseboards
clean, void of anything
but the dirt
gathering in
the corners

only then

do I remember

my walls

have never had

wallpaper

Marley
Xtina Marie

The graveyard was overrun;
it was apparent loved ones
had stopped visiting
years ago

but it was peaceful—

a quietness
I experienced
nowhere else
permeated
the faded script
etched into headstones
and entrances to
cold marble mausoleums

abandoned bouquets
of assorted flowers
and baby's breath
scattered over
the barely-there path,
but I could still
make it out
when the moonlight shone
just right through
the skeletal trees

I sit near a cross,
and trace the name
deeply engraved

into the stone

Marlene Martin
Loving daughter, wife, mother

and a sadness stirs
within me

because I am
a loving daughter, wife, mother

I finger the dainty
gold necklace
with *Marley* inscribed into it
hanging from my neck
and I cry for this stranger
buried 6 feet beneath
where I sit

it's so quiet here

Black Eyes
Xtina Marie

unearthly cries
interrupted the night,
and the rain hid
the sadness
dripping from
black eyes
unwilling to say
goodbye

Oddly Eternal
Xtina Marie

Not every
love story
has a
happily ever after

no sparkly fairytales
or magical sunset walk-offs
as we gaze
lovingly into
each other's eyes

some end in
broken glass
and blood staining
cold tile floors
that may in time fade,
unlike the internal scars
that are… oddly eternal

and

harsh words screamed
in fury,
shattering spirits
that are
much more difficult
to heal
than the bruises
placed carefully
under a light sweater

some love stories
begin as adorable
meet cutes
and accidental
insta loves,
the kind
neighbors and family
talk about as
serendipitous
or meant to be

while ending in
a white knuckled
psychological thriller

ours ended
with the panicked
sounds of screaming,
guttural and animalistic
as I fought for
my sanity
among the empty
liquor bottles
and fragments
of my mind
somewhere buried in
the debris
of an extreme horror novel

our love story
ended
with a bang,
and pain,
the harsh smeared maroon

seeping into
cracks in the floor…
　　oddly eternal

The Funeral of a Fairy Tale
Serena Daniels

Once upon a time,
I believed in love like castles in the sky—
golden towers, whispered vows,
a story written in the stars.

But the carriage was rusted metal,
the glass slippers cracked,
and the prince never rode in—
just a stranger in borrowed words.

The roses wilted before the wedding,
the clock struck twelve too soon,
and love, that fickle spell,
faded like fog at dawn.

So here lies the fairy tale,
buried in the ruins of "once upon a time."
No doves, no ballads, no magic left—
only dust where dreams once bloomed.

Unlucky Love
Tom Duke

I once dated a killer clown. He was a colorful guy, bright and interesting, but my sense of humor just killed him.

On rebound I co-dated conjoined twins but on our first 'double-date' they fought like two dogs over the last scrap of meat. I was initially flattered, but ooh, the flying saliva!

Then there was the mortician. I know, I know, yes he was creepy. Always raised a single eyebrow and talked like Bella Lugosi, and his tongue was not a tongue but a probe. It was quite erotic. At first.

I thought I got lucky when introduced to the dentist. No kidding, he was kind and gentle—to the point of irritation. And always apologizing! I wonder if they've found him yet.

I'm happy to say I have finally met *him*—my true love. He's retired and old, though, and I'm afraid he won't last long. One way or another.

Mine Alone
T.K. Guest

The rasp of that tongue
serpentine and bold

leaves my lucent skin sore,
paper-thin, stained, spoiled

palest vellum of the lamb
written on, indelibly.

So beloved, kept close, I
cannot take that shape

cannot, or will not?

Devotion stilts vestigial wings
withering them with a touch

your coarse heart thrums and you lend me
its carnal rhythm as I lay,
forming.

Impatient, spitting blood, you crawl inside
pray to the formless, clutching hollow bones
in hand

crush them with ease
scatter my ashes
and utter that age-old wish:

omnia vincit amor.

Bitter Winter
T.K. Guest

a branchless family tree
in bitter winter, stripped back
teeth bared, smiling, you speak of
pruning mine with metal shears
my fist splits your lip, you tremble
but not with fear.

knuckles in my mouth, I lie
heaving breaths in the darkness
where no-one, not even I
can see those charcoal thumbprints
you left on my lower back
maybe deeper

pine-scented breaths at my ear
a disguise for the axe-man
eager like the thrum of my
heart, electrical impulse
animating dying flesh
and, well, by god

what is my blood if not just
iron – flowing, forming, a
cog in your machinations
I'd put a bullet in you (I *would*)
if you wouldn't spit it back,
drooling shrapnel

how could anything grow here?
how could a – a family

tree put down
new roots?

mycelium, I whisper
I scream, but nothing comes out.

Love Letters Returned to Sender
Serena Daniels

Dear Me,
I know your heart is already bending,
soft as wax in their heated hands.
You see poetry in their silence,
but trust me—it's just an empty room.

Dear Me,
Stop tracing sonnets in their sighs.
They are not a tragic hero,
just someone who loves the chase,
but never the keeping.

Dear Me,
When they say *forever,*
watch how their lips barely move,
as if the word is borrowed,
never meant to be theirs.

Dear Me,
Burn this before you read it.
I know you won't listen.
You never do.
—Me.

HellBound Books Publishing LLC

She Who Eats Scorpions
C. Payne

The taste of poison,
and caress of claws
is all the comfort she needs.

Bitter solace
crawls down her throat,
she sobs in ecstasy.

Light soon fades,
all thoughts cease
euphoria slowly grows cold.

Let us mourn
for she who eats scorpions,
there's one less ghost in this world.

The Imp and the Fairy Princess
H.L. Dowless

There once was an imp whose appearance was vain,
his behavior was foolish, even his speech and imposing
    mannerisms were maimed!
From those eastern cannibalistic lands afar he and his
kind
    had once been blessed,
indentured to serve the superlative bloods' best.

His mortal salvation was his own indenture,
for in his own lands very few of his age did survive
    the daily adventure,
let alone thrive
    as a simple butler employed in basic mealtime bequest,
being allowed his nourishment from among the tables'
    finest!

For many years with his situation he was quite contented
    until he commenced to keep company with envious
out-landers,
    who told him tales of wealth reserved from his labor
and invented
    more tales of fabulous riches in his own land that his
presence pandered had forced his loss,
callously forgetting his past perilous situation
    and the weight he once bore in carrying his daily cross.

So he cried unto the fairy princess beseeching his complete liberty;
   though at first she denied him his requested delivery,
she promised him that she would grant him his freedom for
   all infinity....
So he continued on in his daily chores inside that lavish
   mansion home,
existing in luxury of living and never alone,
   as the weeks went by, transforming into creeping months in his atone.

As the days passed and so did the weeks,
he was approached by the out-lander, *Rahab*, who
   pretended to offer wisdom
unto those in need who seek.
   Her true desire was to hex with *Chaos* and *Destruction*,
by causing her targeted victim to become malcontent
   in his present position,
desiring the decadence of his past homeland
   o'er the place where in luxury he did presently stand.

"Just observe thyself in that peon's place where ye now
stand,
   ye a wanton servant in another on' 's mansion estate,
when thee once possessed thine own so grand. Dost thou
truly believe that thy owner can afford to allow thee
liberty? My best suggestion then,
   is to put her words to the test,
now wouldst thou not agree?"

"Oh then, let's do see," replied the imp so sheepishly,

"the thought of a lying tongue had never crossed me....
     But I will take your suggestion and you'll never regret
the day that you offered me your very best
     In words and honorable advice."

   "Thou art very attentive to true wisdom's slice,
and thy gain in doing so shall indeed be very nice.
     So approach the dear princess come first glow
tomorrow morn,
     and behold the manner in which her waning
inattentiveness
     shall allow thy new revelations to be born,"
firmly replied Rahab.

     Thus on the first light of next morn,
the imp did make his approaching move;
     his chance taken did cause the dear princess scorn,
her sound derision putting him on the groove.

     Her reply being "next light or maybe the next blushing
sun rise,
     or might be the light following, if the good feeling
should strike;
     but on whose advice do you make your inquiry, unto
one of my adoration
     or my despise?
One of thy disdain or one of honest invite?
     Doth he stand firm among those floundering fools or
tall among the wise?
     For do behold, thy success shall rest on the shoulders
of my personal likes

of both you an' the very moment,
and please do remember that it is unto me no obligation
    anywhere that I should bear binding ties!,"
so stated the dear princess in a resounding reply.

On the twelfth striking in the shadow of the full moon
didst Rahab approach to offer him confidence in success,
    granting him courage to persevere through on the test.
Before she melted from his secular presence,
    she demanded of him another advising spoon,
wishing him her very best,
    neath the light of a full witch moon.

"Fall upon thy knees facing the cold damp earth below,
offering prayers unto thy lording King, Apolyon, for him
to
    bestow
upon thee his fetid blessing, delivering up his sacred
    prince,
the lord of *Chaos, Antagonism and Suspense.* This dark
saint, thence,
    shall then march forward unto the fairy princess,
causing her to feel the forces of dread and woe,
    until she allows thy people and thou the unfettered
liberty to go."

So then the imp heeds her dark words of twisted
knowledge,
    horribly mistaking them for gifted wisdom.
Thus...out in hinter most wilderness graveyard dark
corner,

keeling in homage
to the Lord of Dark Lies and Deceit, pleading unto him in
   his enthroned kingdom
to intercede in his own behalf.
   Thus didst Apolyon's disdaining figure appear from the
thin air,
   demanding that he forbear his request until the light of
the following day had passed.

   "Was it not thee who sought out my relaxing presence?
How wouldst thee dare disturb my rest,
   beseeching me loudly in my very residence!
Even demanding from me my very best!"

   The trembling imp.., now one so terrified,
glanced with wide palled eyes from side to horrifying
side,
   knowing not what to say or even how to reply....
He could only attempt to gaze forth into a face so
   repulsive,
then only hanging his face toward the ground, trying not
to
   sound explosive.

   "Yes the guilty one was I,
though I am not a saint.., sir I can never tell a lie;
   my intention was never to disturb you,
but to beseech only in earnest request.., with a last
gasping
   sigh..,
just to see what it was that thee would then do."

Apollyon laughed in a voice thundering on the raging wind,
then the darkening skies cleared as the streaking lightening went.
The malicious genie then paused with both muscle bound arms crossed,
gazing down upon the poor imp o'er whom he knew himself to be boss.

"Very well," he did thunder, "if thou be brave enough to endure the loss..,
indeed I am most certain that thee hath once pondered and waved all of the cost?
The one whom advised thee to approach and brave the tempest roll,
casually neglected to inform thee.., that my price extracted
shall be thy blundering soul!"

"Oh please, there, Mr. Genie," begged the poor imp. "I am pleading of you just one more attempt
to sway the fairy princess, both very chaste and wise, to let me and my people go, if you could so advise?"

"Very well then," replied the genie, "do as thee feel so led,
but I shall now inform thee that thy forlorn effort is dead;
for the princess' heart is as solid as granite stone,

her concern is preserved for her own extravagant
wealth...
    and let lavish living be her only song.
Thou art only born to exist as her sweat drenched laboring
    mule....
Thy miserable life in her fields shall surly be thy only
    incessant rule."

With the peach rise of the morning sun,
the imp did make his way toward the gardens and the
    vineyard run,
approaching the delicate fairy princess with the question
    hot on his mind,
the answer looming ever still that he was hoping to find.
    In great reverence the imp didst dare to approach,
dropping down upon a single knee in earnest beseech,
    placing both hands together in humble pining bow,
dearly requesting that the princess honor his earnest
    avow.

"Please my dearest Mrs. Xantho,
of my gasping plea thee does surly know
    that I only desire my own freedom of will.
If it is that I should only candidly come Around and go;
    but of thee thou will posses my devoted loyalty still,
I in gracious earnest desire to impart so."

The fairy princess laughed deeply from within,
her face then streaked with a thin waxing grin.
    Her beholding the imp.., donned in perfect dress and
tie,

she could only shake her head in great wonder as to why.

"Whereas thy lavish provider hath now been me,
thy only indenture is unto thee, when it is that thou art
free.
When ye precious suit and tie ye must surly forbear,
what then may ye endeavor to wear..., rag cloth, possum
skin, or hare?
When thy food is caviar, rice, and tender river cane
shoots,
when ye are then forced to forbear, what then may be
thy nourishment...,
carrion, rat flesh, and tuckahaw roots?
What manner of employment shall sustain thee,
when thy only labor hath been in support of this elegant
mansion house
and it's affluent company?"

"None-the-less Mrs. Xantho, please allow my wishes
to be,
my dear heart desires it's passion of will,
for my poor soul yearns only to be free....

Does not the robins desire to cross o'er on high still,
when the fall arrives and the far south is best to be?
Does not the graceful stag choose to roam woods and
open fields,
so that only he may profit from their bounteous yields?
Well in likewise fashion, so do I
desire to go by my own design.
By my own ingenuity any resulting possible wealth
shall be my soul pine.

If all else should fail, Mrs. Xantho,
    then by the rights of my own labor, I shall do just fine."

    The fairy princess did take a deep sigh,
only to shake her golden head in wonder as to why...
    When one lives so well and enjoys life in the shade
that he would choose to abandon all of it for poverty on
    any given day.

    "Well.., so it is that we shall simply just *wait and see.*
On occasion it takes time for the mind to conceive
    the folly that it has come to believe,
when all appears so much better, indeed...,
    from where it is that he stands making his foolish
reprieve."

    Late that night on a stormy twelfth striking the wicked
genie did reappear,
    his haunting spectrum, ever so near.
The imp now came to dread his daunting approach,
    for he knew well that deeply into his breast the evil hand
desired to encroach.

    "Very well then ye foolish imp,
allow thy bumble wishes now to initiate.
    For presently unto me thee hath made thy request.
If ye should ever turn and run, I shall lay thee and all of
    thine to infinite waste.

    Now there is no turning back.

Thy request was the gift of thy infinite liberty and without
     haste...,
and soon the price shall come due unto me of thy most
     treasured best.
Had ye chosen to remain, then ye might have been
     allowed
the granting of another deep silent, most secret debauched
     wish..,
that being the sight of unadorned pastel flesh;
     but since ye have thrown it all away on whimsical
thoughts,
     now there is no turning back to obtain thy corrupting
wants.
     Now have a bit more patience and heed these dire
warnings,
     for soon there shall come a mighty storming
upon the grand estate of the fairy princess.., until the
     moment is right,
then she shall allow ye and all of ye impish kind
     to flee away into the bleak stormy night."

"Oh dear Genie," sighed the imp, "if only I could now
retreat,
     my poor eyes could tingle then with enraptured glee,
for there is no other pleasure that it's good feeling may
     beat
that of my poor eyes beholding chaste pastel flesh..,
     so clean.
So pleasant is the sight to behold, that I shall rhyme song
     and sing;
for it's joy unto my eyes is far greater than that ever to be
     wrought by the precious sound
of sweet freedom's ring!"

So on the ninth night from the genie's last visit
the figure of *Chaos* did move upon the earth bound estate
    to insist
that the hardened heart of the fairy princess reconsider to
    make reprieve,
allowing the imp and his kind to have their unchaperoned
    leave.
Not only that if she still should answer no,
    then the dark curse of *Chaos* would come to fill every
estate
    in the entire land with woe.

    Thus he
being the second out-lander to move with envy
    for the fairy princess stable wealth
in Rahab's wake.
    In the witching moon of the twelfth striking
did Chaos ascend upon the princess gracious estate,
    destroying all the lush gardens and the mansion, as it
may,
    laying all of the lavish fields and stores to waste.
When the imp did again make his approach toward her,
    once more her sharp reply was *"no"* and without haste.

    So again did Chaos move, but this time, to fill the entire
land.
    Laying destruction upon every beast and the labored
works of man.
    Now there existed no restraints upon the imp and those
unfettered brutes of his own kind.

They were at long last free to do according to the whims of their own mind.

But before they all were to have their first dash toward their heart's desire,

there was one more visitor who would appear unto them all,

bearing a brilliant sword of perfect bronze, flaming with dancing mid-night fire.

This visitor was a singing cherub from the supreme one..., so mighty and divine,

who bore a punitive warning with all of them in mind.

"Yes..., do go and roam the earth in search of all that thee and thy vain kind

may chance to find,

but in thy desultory quest for luxury and liberty,

just remember that ye neglected me for

making thy first inquiry.

For all of eternity ye shall thus be reminded of my words.

Do go on and take thy secular pleasures of purloined wealth

and wasted corrupting pastel flesh;

but for the sin of making thy appeal to Satan in bequest,

one day thee and thy kind shall be bound in numbers

greater than ever before heard,

their shackles loudly snapping before ye and thy kind can even pause

to ponder or guess from whence came the wicked bird.

BEHOLD

The entire land shall then be infinitely liberated from thy

noxious girth....
Beware the first lure, which shall be thy profit in absence of
    any transfer in work.
When the second lure shall be a dismantling absence of
    corporate regulation,
the golden twin towers shall soon fall in great
conflagration.
    When the restraints upon the subtle King's authority
shall then see their complete removal,
    his absolute reign shall find it's superior mortal
approval.
Thus I tell ye, that thee and thy kind should tremble with
    trepidation and fear,
for then thy complete damning subjugation looms near."

    After the announcement of these words.., the imp did
move on.
    The pleasures of the moment consumed his heart, soul,
flesh and bone.
    His sons and daughters accept not tomorrows fate,
for their gluttonous debauched desires can no longer wait.
    But so true to the angel's warning reprimand,
the flaming towers have already collapsed so deeply into
    the sand.
 The king in command now bears no restraint,
    that precious doctrine of liberty he will soon move to
taint....
    Then all of the imps shall exist as his own mortal bane,
 his sons and daughters forced once again to live in
chains;
    their impish minds will never comprehend even their
own pain,

living only to gratify an elitist element's insatiable gain.

The good fairy princess...,
though she so sadly wept in her bitter reprieve,
her sons and daughters forced to forgo all excess,
countless numbers choosing to leave.
In the passage of time she once again rose to her feet,
though not yet nearly as strong, appearing somewhat
weak....
She.., despising the debauchery in the world all around her,
schemes to ascend into authority, hoping to remove the poisonous cancer.
In her heart she knows that one day her glorious reign shall somehow again come..,
She feels the celestial promise upon her face every morn
with each rise of the peach sun.

One Night by the Hangman's Tree
LindaAnn LoSchiavo

Despair found me a dozen steps from the hangman's tree dazed by pre-dawn hush, squinting at the bark's myriad imperfections and odd notches, some similar to letters. Wait. Did someone carve *oupire*? Impossible. Yet the word broke through the bastion of my thoughts, its sinister meaning slipping into my awareness like a skilled burglar. My attraction to broken wings, broken men, generated a low drone of dread, my lips parched with dry gloom and unuttered yearning. A moral failing.

A shadow bewitched the branches, thrilling me with a swoop of dark energy. Large footprints impressed the damp turf, great ghost ships of shoes. A tall, lean figure moved towards me, skullish in his gauntness and unworldly pallor, attire too formal for a forest trek. Rivulets of red streaked his stare, eyes all undimmed shock as if staring into questions that are invisible to mortals. Could he detect my goosebumps from my silhouette in poisoned starlight?

Suddenly, he covered my bare shoulders – with the plushest cashmere scarf or cape – saying that we must not keep friends waiting, urgency whispered with a heavy accent, betraying the lisp of a secret woe or ill-fitting dentures.

As my free hand clasped the fabric, my coil of rope slid to the ground. Untethered, I let the stranger usher me through the red moon's mist onto a gravel path as if we'd both made a bargain under our shared sky.

. . . . .
Note: Oupire is the Polish word for vampire.

During Happy Hour at the Undead Lounge
LindaAnn LoSchiavo

After our breakup, right around sunset,
Dan's never coming home again became
My grief o'clock. Then Undead Lounge opened,
Barmen preparing drinks as carefully
As a blood sacrifice. One happy hour,
A stranger bought a round and winked at me,
Eyes dark as soul-sheen ashes. Sitting down
In his booth with my glass, I extended
My palm. Instead of shaking hands, he kissed
It thoroughly, a white mist shadowing

Us both, until we were inside his house.
That cocktail must have … my confusion … how …
His breath felt hot along my ears and neck,

Kite-stringing my emotions as we flew.
Did I black out? Anointing rain obscured
A cemetery. Fading, he became
Mere ghostly fragments as the sun came up.

Lady Madeline Usher's Revenge
LindaAnn LoSchiavo

> *"We have put her living in the tomb!"*
> *– Poe, Fall of the House of Usher, 1839*

Poe's story didn't cover Roderick
With glory, shoving me inside that crypt
Alive though bored to death — shut up, my sole
Companion him, doomed gloomy twin. How droll
To dream he'd benefit — sole ownership —
As if our home, with that décor, was hip:
Dark passages, frayed somber tapestries,
Tarnished armorial mementoes. He's
A hoarder. Junk became his "rare antiques."

Insipid arguments were his technique
For keeping me unmarried and distressed
About his health, discouraging my guests,
Manipulative, daring suicide
Each time I saddled up my horse. A bride
I might have been, a beauty in my youth.

Rod got what he deserved and that's the truth.

Come Softly to Me
LindaAnn LoSchiavo

Homeless, she took to sleeping on fresh graves.
Soft soil and silence lullabied her, wraiths
Less threatening than city rapists, crooks.

Conscience insisted: *offer something back*.
Addiction scorched her voice so she spoke-sang
"Come Softly to Me," staring at a face
Engraved on Ezra Everhart's tombstone,
Just twenty years of age when he was killed,
Aware her ankles were caressed, despite
Being alone. His black soil welcomed her
Body – expecting her, providing warmth,

Considering which soul to rouse by dawn.
Instead audacious moonbeams interfered,
Disguising, then transporting her through thick
Narcotic clouds, a waif wafted on winds.

She woke, surprised to be back on the street,
Remembering love's touch, its secret spell.

Lady Ligeia—Redux
LindaAnn LoSchiavo

Ligeia's what they called her. That barroom
Was known for vices, everything for sale.
I'd wooed that chick with coke, beef jerky, ale
For all her friends. She's single (I'd assumed),
'Til Edgar Poe showed, said he was her "groom."
Inviting him to duel, I watched him pale.
Drama ensued — and thereby hangs a tale.
They're *ghouls*, those two! They'd met inside a *tomb*.

Bloodthirsty Poe bled beauty dry. Pre-doomed
Ligeia, Annabel Lee, and Berenice —
Insidiously felled and pushed offstage —
Had met goth's Mr. Goodbar on the page.
Belles fueled his quill; their death gave him release.
Some vampires kill with ink — refill, resume.

After-bloom
Naomi Simone Borwein

The rough dirty soles of his feet scrape against my
calves.
Brushing against my toes. (The forked cleft of heart
tissue in the marrow).
He rotates back and forth on the bed gaining leverage.
(Thrumming beat.)
I roll off the surface, legs gaited
and I run.
Rapid breath—inhale
(blossoms of amaryllis) panting
cold beads of sweat
on my forehead;
I cannot catch my breath.
Pacing, breath.
A sharp involuntary inhalation.
The air is thickening around me.
(The veins of petaled flesh.)
I can see it condense, particles swimming,
thick in the atmosphere
around me.
He is rolling, towards me:
bouncing, jumping, rotations
(in the out-croft).
A dirty
coloured wire,
tissue clumped around a ruby substance
(of spent flowers and stalks | the garden).

There are steps.
Softer this time.

A door opens;
a head peaks through
a heart-shaped face.

(Valves tightening fine spun chambers
along a path.)

~~I have come to apologize.~~ There is a low growl,
~~I am truly sorry for what I have done.~~
Then the sound of metal puzzle pieces
sliding and clinking.
Shallow breath.
Steps.
The pieces of metal.
Growing softer.
A door opens and closes
Another growl…
(Wild howl of bones)
The clinking muffled.
~~Can I have my blade back?~~
~~Is that the only reason you apologized?~~
~~Ya…~~
~~You aren't sorry at all.~~
~~No.~~
The clicking continues.
The metal pieces swing closer and closer to my face
like the pieces of metal windmill.
A turbine.
Broken.
In his hands.
A cough.
Mumbled lyrics
(carving),
half-singing.

A balloon bounces off my head (sinew).
More growling.
The tinkle of metal like bottles swinging from a tree
Suspended on ropes—like a
haint tree—in the South—
Spirit tree.
A forced laugh,
haaaa haaaa haaa deadening the last syllable
The clinking continues.
Just enough to keep you off kilter.
Sound polluting.
And then the lights come. Ambient
flaring.
The clink now a clang.
Architectured anxiety.
Shifting.
Displaced.
Transposition of sounds and touch and light.

I am dancing on my legs.
Weaving (stalks of warping flowers
skeletal)
proprioception.
Muscles fighting to keep my body together and
coordinated.
I feel weight on my neck, and a pain in my right lung.
(Housed in a prison of granite
on a cliff overlooking the western sea.)
The clanging,
a sound loop starts to play.
The pressure.
I can't breathe.
~~Why can't you just say you're sorry?~~
He shoved his palm into the small of my back hard.

Singing,
Not everything is intentional.
~~*Like your birth. Were you planned in a lab*~~
~~*with all kinds of other creepy things?*~~
The clanging continues.
The metal pieces rotate, inches from my face.
He whispers;
clink clink.
The words are garbled
(petals, whorl spun).
The clinking
~~*You misspelled it you b*tch!*~~
Ahhhaaaa,
Can I touch your xxxx?
    Can I touch your xxxx?
        Can I touch your xxxx?
            Why is xxxx censored?
I say nothing.
His tongue rolls in his mouth
(ichor flooding his palette).
He points the metal paddles at my face,
perched up on a lath of wood glossy resin,
Aaaaahhhhhh.

Do you love me?
His eyes are black.
Do you love me?
I say nothing.
Do you love me? Why don't you love me anymore?
Ahhhhhhhhh… stop.
The spit hits my hands, frigid drops
(ice dripping from the spine),
splayed on dry skin.

My forearm is wet.
(Pooling).

The metal posts are pressing against my cheek;
little points of pain snake in between my jaws.

Good morning sunshine.

My body shudders, my eyelids; and I wake.
The poppyseed-sized hole in the wall is blinking at me.

And close open and close. Rushes in.

This Grave's Kiss
Kevin Hollaway

Pray tell please, what did I miss?

The serene touch of this grave's kiss?

I wasn't expecting sorrow and shame

Yet no one above is calling my name

Do not bury me yet, I have acts to confess

There is much to tell, much to digest

I protest my descent to these depths

But my voice fades, no air is left

In the earth around I hear things creep

Too many secrets are all that I keep

Against this box my nails claw and peel

Longing for you is all that I feel

Fists pound against this velvet bed

This prison of death, this box of dread

Perhaps silence will liberate, and allow me to say

Let my heart scream, before turning to gray.

There you are, I feel your cold hand!

Barely flesh now, bone to sand

They put us together! How sweet and kind!

We can travel now where no one can find.

This bizarre mix of sorrow and pride

Consumes as we lay side by side

Pray tell for what sin, at what cost

Buried us here with all that is lost?

I found you my dear, what did I miss?

The serene touch of your grave's kiss?

HellBound Books Publishing LLC

I Love You Now More Than Ever
Carson Demmans

I loved all of you
Except for your cheating heart
So I cut it out

Morella Newcastle
Mark Mackey

Garbed in a silky blood red gown
A long cloak wrapped around her
Stared with youthful eyes at the castle
it stood dark and forboding
an bleak ornament
topping off a bleak mountain
far off in the distance
rumored to be haunted by
the spirit of Evelyn Gastenmire
cursed to be damned for eternity for the act of
hurdling herself off the top of it in despair
her pair of offspring daughter and son
stricken down with dread consumption
before they could blossom into adulthood
she trembled with unparalled fear over this
the gallop of her horses hoofs
pounding on hardened ground
filling her ears
strenously pulling the carriage
she was contained in.
Attending the lavish masquerade ball
was of more importance
Unbeknownst to her
For some unknown reason
she sensed this was her last journey
Yet, she traversed on with a brave heart
This night would be her last

Rope
Edward R. Rosick

Gnarled
brown
leathery,

A weathered
piece of
sinew
that rubbed
the ground as
they walked
apart.

No longer was
it
gorged with
life,
pulsating with
breath
and blood.

It fed
neither.
It consumed
both.

Her fingers
rubbed
it tenderly.
His teeth
tore at

it savagely.

Neither dared
to sever
it.

She called it
a link.
He called it
a chain.

They both
washed it
carefully at night

in the silence
of their bed,

where the rope
entered
each fragile
body

at an
oblique angle.

Game You Call Love
KH

I was just another face lined up
On your wall of conquests
I never imagined I would be like the rest of them
That I would fall for every single fucking thing you said
That I believed it was different with me
And you'd tell me that while telling another
And another
And another
But as long as you told me first...
It didn't really matter
You just put me above them all
Or so I thought
I was really just your voodoo doll
I was blinded by your black magick
And each pin you stuck in me with voodoo hands
But now they're falling out one by one
I was just another conquest
In the game you call love

Burn Your Memory
KH

I set fire to the bridge between us
As I walked away from what you left me
It wasn't much but a handful of useless promises
Long ago broken and scorned
I made sure that boats would capsize
In treacherous waters of pain and anguish
So you couldn't reach me from your side of the split
And there are monsters that thrive beneath the waters
My monsters
They will never allow you to swim to me
Because they know I'm not strong enough
To stay away myself
Because I learned nothing from it all
I still crave to hear your voice whisper
Those carnal sins you ravaged my ears with
So I have to keep the fire going
To ensure the bridge can never be repaired
Which isn't hard for my soul to do
It's been on fire, smoldering
Burning deep into my bones
Burning deep into my thoughts
Burning deep into me
Burning deep into my heart
And it won't take much to reignite the flames
So I can burn your memory, once again, away

You're Not Going to Get Away from Me

Juleigh Howard-Hobson

Carefully, I take some hairs out of your

brush, knot them together. You will

feel my pain.

I pull the knot tighter, until

the strands start to break. My fingers grow sore:

feel my pain

feed my rage. I rip apart your essence,

let it fall in pieces, can you

feel my pain

grow? Can you feel its hot presence?

You're never getting free. You're going to

feel my pain.

Lemons
Samantha Hawkins

I hate the smell of lemons.
The grooves, their texture, remind me of your hands.
The smell reminds me of the last time that I was free.
And I wonder, will I feel anything when you finally die?
Will I weep?
Will I rejoice?
Will I scream in anger at the things left unsaid?
At the bed that's been unmade?
Your existence is a burden that only I carry.
Closure is a myth and time doesn't heal all wounds.
They constantly ooze and bleed over this body of mine
that begs to be rid of you but you're still breathing.
And I'm still stuck in a limbo
I'm not sure even your death will break.

Silent Screams
Candace Nola

Silent screams issue from the voice in my mind.
Reverberating through flesh, marrow and bone, Through
salt laden tears.

Waking old fears, the same, the new,
the forsaken, forgotten, the always dismissed.

Do you
Do you
Do you

A heartbeat sound.
Two words.
It echoes in space

Do you
Do you
Do you

Shattering the windows that only her mind can only seek
out.
Captive. Trapped. Alone in this zone.
Overloaded. Overwhelmed
Drowning in pain

Silent misery she can no longer voice
She screams on her knees
Sinking, loathing, raging in self hate
What more do you need
What else do I lack?

Do you
Do you
Do you

The heartbeat, her heartbeat, echoes back
All consuming hurt, emotional fears.
Grieving again, her soul rents fresh tears
Weary.

So weary
So tired of pain
She sinks in the blackness
Tar covered pitch
She drowns
She stills
No fight left to give

Do you
Do you
Do you

Heart beat. Her heartbeat, Echo covered tears.

Do you
Do you
Do you
Love me back.

Silence is deafening
She gets her reply
Eyes close
Wounded and bloody
She gives up and lets go

Silently dying in the abyss
Do you

Nothing More
Candace Nola

I am woman, nothing more, a secret in the dark.
A mindless empty training hole for man to expel his
youth.
A thing to be used for lust and need and egotistical
growth.

I am woman, nothing more, a chamber for his seed.
A birthing pit for more of him, in servitude of greed.
I am less than he, less than he will ever be,
even dead within the ground. I am soft and
weak, and of simple mind. Nothing more
than an object to be silenced, tamed, and bound.

I am a melody behind background noise,
a presence meant to soothe. I am to nurture,
to feed, to clean, to relieve his every strain.
I am woman, never more. I have no needs of my own,
no voice he needs to heed.

I am woman, raging deep, sick of sorrow and shame.
The fury of gods boils within, the anger of generation
s rises. A female voice meant to be heard, feared
and desired. I am woman, nothing more,
time for men to cower at my fire.

Mother, daughter, sister, aunt, grandmother,
matron, goddess rise. Wake, and stand,
open your eyes. Own the power of your name.
I am woman now, with nothing more
than all the universe to claim.

Echoes
Candace Nola

Memories haunt melodies trapped in a frenzied mind.
 Undulating, unfurling, stretching throughout time.
A life endured in servitude, buried under pain.

Music haunts her, a soundtrack to her shame.
Every note reminds her of who she became.
Lyrics wound the fractured soul, words that scar and maim.

Memories drift in a sea of pain, over every tear stained page.
Watch her closely now, an orchestrated charade.
Watch the show upon the stage, a beautiful facade.

The music lifts, she starts to smile, dropping to a bow.
The trumpets rage, she screams aloud as horns begin to blow.
Raging winds shriek her pain. No turning back now.

The symphony lifts and brings the rain.
The choir sings, an ethereal cacophony
floating in her sea. She sinks deep,
drowning in the ocean her choir has set free.

Her tears have lived a thousand lies,
left her fractured, a soulless thing.
No music left, only echoes remain.
Sounds of sorrow fluctuate as she slowly dies.

Aqua Tofana
Sara Martinez

A drip, a drab,
Dropped in his drink.
Soon on a slab,
Over the brink.

When a husband is wicked
And mistreats his wife,
Take this marvelous liquid
To soon end his life.

If you should wield this power
And use it quite well,
Just allow it to flower
You'll send him to Hell.

It starts first with the coughing
He'll feel rather ill;
His frame full sore and sobbing
And racked with a chill.

Next comes the retching and flux,
His bowel all afire.
When there's nothing left but a husk,
At last, he'll expire.

But pay heed to your mourning,
Let no one suspect
That you hastened his ending.
Show only respect.

Know that one day the Reaper
Comes calling for you.
There's no stalling with prayer
The cost that comes due.

Worth it to know
You sent him first
To the fate sowed,
By himself cursed.

A Demon
Alexander Skubich

A demon whispers things into my ear
Dark things that fuel my fears
They burrow deep into my brain
He speaks of terror, doubt, and hate
Makes me believe he's sealed my fate!
I hate myself for being weak
But everything's so very bleak
I lack the strength to shut him out
He's been with me for so long
The demon grew so very strong!
Shall I drill holes into my head?
Lobotomize away the dread?
He laughs as if he likes the thought
Suggests I take a razor to my throat
Is it time to pen my farewell note?
But wait, I cannot let the demon win
Can't stand his smug and evil grin
Instead, I crawl towards the light
Kill myself I never will
There's hope and laughter in me still!

Through the Forest
Alexander Skubich

"This is just an ordinary night,"
Was my mantra
As I was driving through the forest
But the lights were dim
Headlights only flickering
Painting monsters everywhere
Seen only through
The corners of my eyes
And the shadows grew long
So much longer than usual.
Trees like waiting ghosts
On both sides of the road
Dark and silent
Waiting…
Leaning in
Closer and closer
Threatening to crush me
Grinding me down to nothing
And the darkness grew blacker
So much blacker than usual.
Suddenly eery noises
Echoing around me
Scary, unreal
Making my skin crawl
Creaking wood
Scraping, snapping, crashing
Branches drumming
On the roof, the hood
And the moon shone bright
So much brighter than usual.

Streets so narrow
Twists and turns
Blocking my escape
Trapped in looming shadows
Headlights swallowed up
Just shadows in the dark
Dancing, laughing
Chasing me
And the road kept twisting
Twisting much more than usual.
Speedometer amping up
Faster, faster!
Until...
Glaring light behind a bend
No chance to stop
Instant impact
Metal crashing into metal
And the end came quick
So much quicker than usual.

Rising from the Ashes
Shawna Renée Lewis

I fell deep into
the darkness
and kept falling.
Nothing and no one to stop me.
I found myself in hell
with the numbness
overtaking me.
It was claiming who I was.
Only a cut so deep
by my hand
could make me wake.
No fairytale prince
to kiss me awake.
Just a pain so deep
and unsettled.
When I woke
I realized that my prince
you were not.
I said no!
You set me on fire,
with words that could destroy me,
thinking that I would dissolve.
But,
witches don't burn!
We rise from the ashes
and take flight.

Terminal Lucidity
Chantell Renee

It's dark down there.

Dark and stale.

From here, I see the tiny trails the mealworms have left.

If I follow one, will the insect have hatched into the ebony beetle, or will the plump, soft body of the worm still be there, ready to greet me?

I miss the coolness of the dirt.

Not that I need it yet, but it's nice knowing it's there, waiting.

Yes, there is sun here and smiles and laughs and things I don't think bring joy, but people still smile.

I smile back. Why wouldn't I? In the end, that cold embrace is waiting for them too.

If only it could be a final place to rest, but there's no rest for the twisted.

Not for the divinely fucked.

We are gods of discomfort, lords of distorted perspectives.

Come to think of it, perhaps we've brought some of that stillness with us up here?

Contaminated, we plow through the days ready to see red and bring down the speckles of death in us upon the heads of anyone who dares to be near.

Seems more likely than eternal rest, don't you think?

Off Beat
Chantell Renee

Our cadence is off.

Our hearts that beat in time, convincing us we were human, slowed and sped up simultaneously.

Blood dripped into our sights, coating our worlds in animosity for anyone else with two legs.

How does a heartbeat differ enough to fill you up with the need to thrust both hands into a chest and pry open ribs wide enough to glare at the pumping wet organ?

What about the need for a better life forces you to think of ways to rip a family apart, separated by miles that will turn into lifetimes of nightmares?

How many of our dead need to be floating in flood waters, half eaten in rivers filled with deadly creatures, before we all realize the pulse doesn't need to twin?

How will any of these stolen rights make your life any better? Or are you simply that insignificant that you must leave a bruise with every encounter?

You get back what you put out and trust that the pendulum is panting to swing in full force back the other way. So keep pulling it, higher and higher.

We too are sick of the between beats.

Pump, pump, pum…

Demonic Lullaby
Chantell Renee

Deep down in the darkness
Is where he dwelled
A young boy's spirit
Trapped in Hell
He cried out every night
Got nothing in return
The King of Darkness
Left him there to burn
He was not forgiven
He was not forgot
He was their little toy
They left to Rott

Honey
Chantell Renee

I'm done listening to that sweet honey dripping from your lips.

Those heavy drops are poisonous to my heart.

Each word clogs my future with your misleading intentions.

My thoughts are gooey with images you're not capable of enduring.

You have rotted my dreams.

My time is wasted with efforts used in glazing over our twists and turns.

I've broken through misconceptions most of my life.

Surviving the decay of treachery which drew me to you

I felt the void inside of you, one very much like my own.

My sugar tooth is my weakness.

It must be pulled.

Can this be easy, being a collector of disappointment?

Only here in my sentimental cosmos, among the spiral shavings from the pretty pictures of the life we will never have can I see the damage your sticky words have done.

How could you be so fragrant yet empty?

But I know,

You only secrete this strong taste to overlay the bitterness of your lack in consideration.

I am done absorbing your tacky words.

One cannot fill a hole with more emptiness,

No matter how decadent the taste.

My Realm
Renee Chantell

Here inside I find my discomfort rather comforting.
I know the plains in which I have traveled, this land has
birthed me many lessons.
Layers of ebony disappointment taint my visions of that
I long to see.
For years I have roamed and found no solace, not even
in becoming that which I loathed has ceased this eternal
ache.
I sank far beneath the surface; weighted yet not gone.
Until I find the mirrors and smoke of the whips I have
endured, these shackles remain unbroken.

Parted Fingers
Chantell Renee

Eyes staring up through parted fingers.
Too many questions to move or stay.
Life has made me skeptical, yet a genius at second guessing.
Who do you think I am?
In that trailer park so long ago
Their eyes always colored with anger and neglect.
No one could see, nor did they wish to look
It's hard not to see life through those manufactured windows.
Strange how you can fail yourself so young.
You see, you can choose to drown or swim
I chose to swim, but I'm choking on water filled memories.
Pictures I must push through, rarely spotting dry land.
Fists and loud voices left their own solutions
Twisted broken thoughts to sort it all out with
So, I sit, eyes staring up through parted fingers.
Praying I will soon learn how to float.

The Wonders of Sound II
Chantell Renee

In a state of mental paralysis, I lay and listen
Sounds trigger memories that wash away all thoughts,
sticking me in another time.
One after the other, linked only by similarities, the
pictures submerge me into the past.
Folding me between impressions of cruel hands and
disappointment, I am lost.
Titanic shifts stuff me into an image I can't shield my
eyes from
Sunshine warms my child's face; my pudgy hand
reaches for the dog.
Shrieks of child laughter, flashes of the green of the
lawn, the grey of the steps, the black of his heart.
Those thoughts always lead to him. My monster.
The thief of my innocence and peace of mind.
I try to find the dog, his name was boy, he licked me and
made me laugh.
Please, let me just think of the pup, but my mind starts
again, twisting me into the depths of the rank distortion
of a childhood.
In the pitch blackness it's easier to see the pain than it is
to hold onto the pleasure
What else is there for me to do attached to this decay?
My mind is strong, but my brain is cold.
My heart holds its shape but doesn't deliver fluids like it
once did.
Most of my muscles are dry, stretched over bone that
pokes through peeling skin.
I am alive but not living.

I will remain here until I build up a thirst to animate
again.
Or the dark gets quiet.

Love of My Life
Christian A. Davila

She said, "I love you. How could you do this?"
I gave her a kiss and walked away,
Even though I wish I could have stayed.
No parades or parties for the fallen.
Even though we're done, she wouldn't stop calling.
It was getting heavy—
A month ago, she was my baby.
I was crazy in love; couldn't get enough; better than
drugs, but…it wasn't enough.
I wasn't feeling it.
How can you explain that to someone without killing their
spirit?
I'd fight it more than fear it
And blame it on my indecision,
But the problem made divisions
in the rest of my life. I couldn't take her up as my wife.
No, sir. When it comes to that I have to be sure, and I
wasn't.
Sorry, but I couldn't be a husband.
I had to get away, so I chose to run away.
Break-ups are fierce, but you can't just play
with emotions. I had no devotion, so it wasn't working.
The next month, I paid a visit. Thinking she was over it.
I knocked on the door—no one opened it.
I knocked again. No one opened again.
I thought about it…then, I let myself in,
Thinking, *I've been here a million times.*
It's fine. No one ever minds.
So, it's no biggie. I moved past the chimney, up the stairs,
then started reminiscing

About the times we had. Things were good and bad, just like anything.

I started practicing, in my mind, going over everything.

I wanted you, so I came to see if you wanted me back too.

I walked in her room—it was dark.

I hit light switch, the lights twitched with a popping spark.

She wasn't there; I wondered where she could be.

Suddenly, I saw a whole lot of troubling things.

A large shrine, candlelit, with pictures of me.

I said, "Oh, my God." Then, I was out before I noticed someone behind me.

Woke up in a dark room, unfamiliar.

On a cold floor, chained to a pillar.

This place was like a dungeon men hung in with doubt, upside down with their insides out.

All around was a pungent odor that permeated with a strong taste that made me think of despair.

The last thing I wanted to feel in that lair; I woke up in a nightmare I couldn't bear!

I calmed myself down. I knew I had to get out, but I didn't know how.

I started thinking and thinking; my mind kept blinking back to how I got there.

Then, it became all too clear when I saw her face appear.

She smashed my shoulder with a hammer.

I clamored in pain, yelled and exclaimed,

"What's going on?!"

She yelled back, "What's going on?! Your love is all gone!

That's what's driving me crazy!"

"Crazy?! That's an understatement, baby!

On top of that, I need you to hear me out!"

But she wouldn't hear me out; she just tuned me out

By yelling out loud and smashing, smashing

Consciousness started collapsing before she stopped smashing.

She was getting tired.

I was adrenaline-wired, body burned like fire, about to expire.

I looked over at the love of my life across that desolate place.

Examined her desolate eyes, her desolate face.

This was the last taste, so I drank it in.

When she was going to hit me again,

I'd shimmied loose and grabbed her hand.

I spun her around, heard a slam,

And said, "DAMN! If you had only listened to me...now, you can't."

I broke her mouth, told her I loved her, kissed her softly, looked up to my God, and said, "I can't..."

I wouldn't make it to the hospital if I ran,

So, I turned back to her...and then, I began.

The East Wind
Don Liddick

The wind howls its lamentation, soulless
The sound, or else a woeful miser's moan,
Unwilling to grant a boon or to bless
The night-watch with lull or sigh. A bleak tone,
Unmindful to refresh or give caress,
When from 'nor-eastern blast heart's hope is flown.
'Tis the inverse of melody or song,
An anthem to break the meek and the strong.

On this wild eve, a man chooses a tale
From the shelf a bound tome to enthrall.
No way to suspect he soon will grow frail
From words contrived to inspire his hope's fall.
A dext'rous Muse to spawn such a wail
Expressive of love fled, gone past recall.
So doleful the story, one might well guess
The author's aim was to cry and confess.

Reader hunkers down and tabby curls round
His feet slippered and warmed by fire flaming.
Groaning, the east wind slings sleet on the ground
And pelts windows like bone-roller gaming.
Engrossed by the tome, the man has soon found
A strong need for his fear to be taming.
A confession indeed, a madman's creed—
Dire images in his mind it does breed.

Gripping the binding, he guesses the end—
No, it's more like foresight or clear vision.
Good wife in the book was driven to wend

Her way with adulterous concision.
The husband, no better, still would not lend
Mercy, but acted with calm precision:
A lass lovely was hacked and dismembered,
Vowed the fiend, "She'll not be remembered!"

Arch-backed tabby skitters off with a hiss
When the reader flings foul tome to the fire.
His heart skips beats with the world all amiss,
And the wind wails like some infernal choir.
With mind near toppled, he recalls a kiss,
And decries his Accuser as liar.
Yes, he'd killed his wife, in exact fashion,
Just like in the book—a beast of passion.

An epilogue there was—one he'd not read—
Comeuppance, of sorts, was just to instate.
(He'd feared his madness would dearly be fed
By the grim writings the sheafs would relate).
But sanity soon will be put to bed,
What he feels surely, one cannot conflate:
His life and the book, one and the same,
And what will come next, a hell-ghoulish game.

It comes back in a rush—*He* wrote the book
And buried the truth in his mind twisted;
Knowing what's next and so afraid to look,
Or to full own with what he had trysted.
Devil's deal had seemed good, nor could he brook
A wife's revolt from his love, tight-fisted.
Lovely and dark, her blood sluiced down the drain;
Worth it! thought he and worshipped at fane.

But now the last chapter is Satan's joke,

An item grave indeed. There was a clause,
Fine print in the pact—up gone in blue smoke.
Our author in earnest signed it because
Much was to gain from a hasty pen's stroke;
But due is the bill, Doom slithers and crawls.
Gibbers a night voice, a sound of foul glee:
Devil is greedy and will have his fee.

Dim are the embers, the wind moans quite low.
Now, dare to behold the thing that appears!
Not ghost or wraith with chain clinking in tow,
But carnal beast to collect on arrears!
She slops down the hall, on him to bestow
The consummate of all stark-wilding fears;
It's his wife's body parts imbued with life,
To give and take and feast full on old strife.

A headless torso slithers its approach,
Impelled by desire, of him to implore.
One might guess her aim was less to reproach
Than a query make he could not ignore.
Now here rolls her head, on him to encroach—
Mad man gibbers, no will left to restore.
Lips pale speak (husband's sanity long fled):
"Come hither my love, and then we to bed!"

No riches from book sales nor vengeance cold
Can balance out our author's mind madness.
Let us slip the veil o'er horrors untold,
Or would you see her head's kiss with gladness?
No, it is enough, we need not be bold,
But should ruminate love's loss with sadness.
One flesh united, the east wind still blows,

And cares not for love or man's wailing woes.

We Were All the Rave
Rebeka Goodman

The last funeral I braved was a cremation—
a crude word, unfit for such a rite.
"Wake," perhaps, lets sorrow dress for the occasion.

On a parched February morning, I got the call.
In lieu of flowers,
I brought a portrait I painted—
of you, as I remembered,
before the accident.

Met you when I was eighteen,
called you my best friend
till I was nearly thirty.
I was the first one there
and the last person you called.

You would've hated the way they made you look—
and the cheesy ballads they chose.
I kept watching the door,
expecting you to pull up—
playlist ready,
a full tank of gas.

We were all the rave.
We watched the sunrise
as we danced the night away.
It feels so wrong to be at your wake.
We went together like acid and base.
It feels obscene to stand so still
within your eulogy.

Someone called your passing
a bitter blasphemy.

The pastor read a psalm.
Your little sister told a story
about the time you fixed her bike.
They said you were kind.
Someone said you were reckless.
I tried to punch them with my eyes.

But no one said
how you hated tomatoes,
how you gave the best hugs,
had the biggest heart.
They missed your arms like architecture
the shelter in your chest—

I whispered your favorite joke
into my cupped hand
and dropped it in with the dirt.

They told me grief softens.
But they didn't say
it goes quiet first—
hollows your body
and waits there.

I left the portrait leaning against the wall.
I hope there is justice in the afterlife.

Night Shadow
Shawna Renée Lewis

I walk through the night
cold and broken.
My withered body just
a shadow of who I use to be.
The night is my shade,
from the harsh lights
of reality.
My only refuge from the living.
I am chained to no one
but myself now.
I prefer it that way.
It is worth the trade.

Your Prison
Shawna Renée Lewis

I lay black roses on your grave
Knowing
that your coffin
is made of iron
and soaked with holy water.
This gives me peace.
Now you are the one trapped
till you are no longer
even a whisper on the wind.
Your prison for eternity.

Ne'er-do-well
Diane Bright

As he stood before her,
Snarling in that way,
All she could think was
Ne'er-do-well, why won't you go away?

She works hard a toiling,
Stacking hay each day,
But no hand does he offer
Ne'er-do-well, why won't you go away?

The self-indulgent fool,
Strips her life away,
She can hardly stand it
Ne'er-do-well, why won't you go away?

Drops of deadly nightshade,
To help him on his way,
This night, she swears woe betide
Ne'er-do-well, you will go away!

But Rage
Kirsten Noelle Craig

So much rage.
So little space in my body for it all.
Bulging, full to bursting.
The uncomfortable sensation
Of ribs cracking,
Organs rearranging,
Blood boiling under the pressure.
Until there is nothing left to speak of
But rage.

Lumbricus Anxieties
Kirsten Noelle Craig

Tiny worms of fear,
Wriggling beneath your
Consciousness.
"But what if no one will
Ever really love you?"
The worms whisper.
Eventually, it's difficult to tell
If the words are from you or
Somewhere else.
And would it even matter if
They were?

The Breaking
Kirsten Noelle Craig

Let me break where no one will
See me.
Let me spring out into
Oblivion.
Darkness finally consuming.
The little control laid to rest
Alongside the murky depths of
My sanity.
Allow me to come undone
Completely.
I've held it all in for far
Too long.

Razor Sharp

Kirsten Noelle Craig

I hold your name in my throat.
A secret.
A curse.
All I can taste is blood.

A Succubusian Tryst
Max Bindi

May the bewitching fragrance of her long raven hair
stop its perfidious encroachment on my senses.
May the vicious enchantment of this moment
be broken once and for all.
For something beyond devilry is afoot.
A sultry breeze comes from afar
languid like the dying wave
that touches the stygian shore
without ever vanishing.
This decadent and serpentine zephyr
creeps into my room surreptitiously
animating the creases of the curtains
like a vague breath of charm.
Imperceptible at first
it caresses my shivering skin
and whispers to my enchanted ears
gradually assuming the semblance
of a woman of fearful beauty.
And I hardly believe myself awake
entranced by her glowing eyes
and insinuating scent.
I succumb to the unearthly allure
of her uncanny influence
letting her long arms
close around me
her seductive mouth slither on my neck
biting deep into my unconscious
blending horror and desire
engulfing my feverish frame
into an infernal vortex of accursed passion.

Until buried into the sweltering coils
of her marvelous shapeshifting body
gasping in need of air
I glimpse through the sensual fog of this sorcery
the superb flick of her forked tongue
that lasciviously licks my blood
from her voluptuous upper lip
to reiterate as if there were any need
my impotence and that of my prayer.

I Left the Light on for Nobody
Megan Macaila

The bulb glowed quietly in the dark, painting the walls
with its soft shadow

Waiving at the cars that passed by, and each hour grew a
little more golden

As if it hoped that the warmth alone would summon
someone home.

The air is thick and unclaimed inviting any poor soul who
might wander in.

Some nights I reach for you maybe out of habit or hunger
or both

But every night my hands only close in on emptiness

And emptiness refuses to hold me back

The light sings a quiet hymn way into the morning

I leave it on anyway

Because leaving it on is easier than admitting no one is
ever coming home

I Want to Hear the Rain
Megan Macaila

Let the window open, I want to hear the rain

Plunge into my mezzanine and wash out all the stains

It's far too quiet here, please turn my records on

These days I dance alone, for everyone I know has gone

He still sits there in his favorite chair, silent as the grave

Oh God, I want to dance again with the man I could not save

Let my window open, I want to hear the rain

For they are tears that he has wept for me

Until we meet again

Give me till tonight for I'll put my soul to rest

An everlasting slumber with a bullet in my chest

Our souls will meet at heaven's gate

Free from all our pain

And always will our bodies rest

Listening to the rain

Nobody's Baby Now
Megan Macaila

Only when I drink
does the clock click once
and the night fold in on itself.
My walls remember a thousand voices,
but none of them are mine.
I left the window open,
hoping the storm would drown you out,
but the wind slipped through the cracks
of our lies,
carrying the taste of you
on its tongue.
I'm nobody's baby now.
Only when I drink
does that shadow where you stood
begin to skip and sway
dancing to a song only we hear.
My only companion in this life
is the shadow in my corner
that isn't even there.
I'm nobody's baby now.
Bring back my memories;
they were not yours to keep.
Bring back the screaming
silence is no way to sleep.
Wash my blood out of the carpet.
You must have loved me.
How could you not,
when you took all of me with you?
When the sun creeps back into the valley,
as though the moon scolded her

and hurt her feelings,
I remember once again:
I am nobody's baby now.

Selfish Ways
Megan Macaila

Forgive me and my selfish ways
You know I can't resist
Forgive me for my stubborn ways
My ignorance was bliss

Forgive me for not loving myself
And hurting those who cared
Forgive me for the joy that's gone
And the pain I cannot bear

Forgive me for my absence
You know how hard I tried
Forgive me for the tears
I tried so hard to hide

Forgive me for my selfish ways
This is all I ask
By the time you read my letter
Another soul has passed.

Broken Doll
Heather Lane

Time–
It moves by so slowly
When you're small.

But–
The bigger you grow
The faster it flies.

Yet–
Somehow I feel as if
I'm in suspended animation.

Cursed–
To watch time go by
For everyone but me.

Stuck–
Sitting like a broken doll
Set long forgotten upon a self.

Boxed–
With all of the other
Obsolete by gone items of the past.

Buried–
Like a time capsule
Just waiting to be found.

Hoping–
One day to be noticed

Amongst the rickrack.

Chosen–
To be a treasure
And not just a dusty old relic.

Never–
To be left broken
Upon the shelf again.

Small
Heather Lane

Small–
I feel incredibly small.
When I was a child
 and felt this way,
 I would
 escape–
Into my make believe world.

Safe–
I was safe
 inside the confines
 of my closet.
Sitting on the cushiony carpet
 that no one had walked upon.
With just the slide of the door,
 I closed myself into my special place.

Dark–
There was comfort in the darkness.
Just me and my imagination
 within the quiet space.
Now as an adult,
 I lay here in my bed
 in total darkness.
It's similar, yet not quite the same.

Small–
I feel incredibly small.
The weight of adulthood problems
 keep crashing down on me

making me smaller and smaller.
I'm afraid that if this load gets any heavier,
 I'll disappear entirely…

Safe–
Is there anyone out there?
Anyone at all?
That will make me feel safe
 like I did as a child?
I don't want to disappear
 into the…

Dark–

Now Sleep
Heather Lane

I lie alone
Sideways–
Across my Queen sized bed
Feeling incredibly small.

Neither my feet
Nor my head
Dangle off of this
Makeshift cloud.

It's just me
Floating–
In the darkened void
That is my room at 2am.

Alone–
With my thoughts.
A dangerous game to play
As everyone else slumbers.

No crickets chirp–
No hum of cars on the highway–
No roar of airplane engines overhead–
Not even a train whistle off in the distance–

Silence–
Only my inner voice
Can be heard
Over the deafening tranquility.

Shhhh–
Please let me sleep.
Please I beg of you–
I need sleep.

The tiny voice
Inside of me cries out–
What's wrong with me?
Does he even miss me?

Ugh!
Stop this now!
Sleep–
It's been a month.

A lump forms in my throat
The tiny voice continues
I can't turn my feelings off that quickly!
I miss him …

Don't you start–
Please don't.
I've cried too many tears
I just want to sleep …

But … I miss him–
Does he think about me?
Was I not smart enough?
Not pretty enough?

Shhhh–
Stop–
I don't know?!
I wish that I did!

My stomach clenches
Hot, heavy tears fall
Like rivulets of molten steel
As I curl into a ball.

I miss him too–
Sleep now–

Fated
Heather Lane

Run,
Virginia,
Run.
The
Wolf
is
coming
your
way.

Run,
Virginia,
Run.
He's
caught
your
scent,
do
Not–
delay.

Run,
Virginia,
Run.
low–
deep–
growls
means
it's
time

to
play.

Run,
Virginia,
Run.
The
Fates
have
stepped
in,
you
must
obey.

Run,
Virginia,
Run.
There's
nowhere
to
hide
the
moonlight
betrays.

Run,
Virginia,
Run.
At
the
edge
of
the

forest,
don't
be
led
astray.

Run,
Virginia,
Run.
The
game
will
soon
end.
When?
Is
for
you
to
say.

Run,
Virginia,
Run.
The
Wolf
is
coming,
this
has
all
been
edgeplay.

Run,
Virginia,
Run.
Fates
have
sent
your
mate.
Time
to
stop
running
away.

Run–
Virginia–
Run–
Into
the
strong
arms
of
your
lupine
swain.

Wait For Me
Heather Lane

Little legs pump
The pedals.
With all their might.
Gotta move them faster.

Faster–

Training wheels skid
Back and forth.
Gotta catch the big kids.
Wait for me.

Please–

At the corner,
The little legs
Come to a screeching halt.
They can go no further.

Marooned–

Left on the island
Of her own block
Because she isn't allowed
To cross the street alone.

Tagalong–

That's all she'll ever be
To the big kids.

Her big sister said,
She had to keep up.

Idolize–

She just wants to
Go wherever she goes,
Do whatever she does,
Someday she will.

Friendship–

Children grow up.
Sisters become
more than siblings.
They become best friends.

Trials–

Sisters are supposed to
Grow up together,
Then become
Wrinkly old ladies together.

Tragedy–

Standing in a hallway
Not allowed to cross the threshold.
Hearing her big sister's heartbeat stop.
Another place she cannot follow.

But–

Many, many years

From now
When her time comes,
Wait for me–

In Loving Memory of my sister Jennifer
9/9/72~6/1/17

A Rhyme of Screaming Silence
Gerina Dunwich

Words ooze from my spirit
Like blood from deep-cut wounds,
Forming something formless
Like music notes untuned.
Each a Sphinx-like riddle,
A hieroglyph, a rune,
the fading rays of sunsets
Devoured by heartless moons.

Memories are daggers,
Dreams a two-edged blade,
Love a poison flower,
Its beauty soon to fade.
Rhymes dance like a graveyard,
A skeleton parade,
From the screams of silence
My poetry is made.

Non Compos Mentis
Gerina Dunwich

Pallid lips slacken, sallowed eyes blacken,
darkness returns like a grim bird of prey.
Chemical kisses, numbness dismisses
thoughts pixelated in disarray.

Words like Black Masses, cracked looking glasses
strip her soul bare in the dead of the night.
Green witches speak, letting doom leak,
Writhing like earthworms blinded by light.

Sanity splatters, mad as a hatter
touched in the head by a quicksilver bane.
Grief everafter, even her laughter
sounds like a scream when the fumes
    kill the pain.

Rise and Fall
Gerina Dunwich

Rise and fall as the silver morning light
Sweeps away dreaming shadows of the night.
Dawn reborn, conjures mirth and metaphor;
Rise and fall like a million times before.
Gentle touch, a cicada singing breeze;
Subtle smile, dancing lips are windswept leaves.
Rise and fall as the oceans ebb and flow;
Heed the call when the blossoms turn to snow.
Then no more shall the silver morning light
Ease my fears and the tears of yesternight.

Tuesday
Xtina Marie

Tuesday
9 miles one way
parking in the employee lot
I'll never find my car later
sandpaper tongue
legs asleep from sitting so long
I think the guy over there is homeless
waiting
hours pass
lady on the hospital phone *still*
too scared to cry
when do I call his mom? do I wait?
finally something, some news
directions to the ICU
could be directions to Syria for all I know
more waiting
doctor with the kind, gentle eyes
heart attack heart attack heart attack
paddles, blockage, stent, aFib
12%, 25%, very lucky
cold ICU room
awake, but disoriented
would she stfu about her damn ice cream
insides shaking
adrenaline falling
stomach pains
am I hungry? what time is it? when did I eat last?
bruised hands
beeping machines
I should have worn a different shirt

leaning over cold rails to kiss goodbye
nighttime
asking hospital security for help
relief to see the red convertible
dear Lord, please let me get home okay
walking up to the darkened house
dogs barking, Rosie screeching
cleaning up the mess
leftovers in the fridge
FRIENDS on the tv
exhausted but not tired
cold sheets
alone

Beautiful Tragedies Vol I

Only through dark poetry can a tragedy become something truly beautiful.

"Beauty is in the eye of the beholder." This phrase has origins dating back to ancient Greece, circa 300 BC; proving that some humans have always had the ability to see beauty where others could not.

Beautiful Tragedies is a compilation of 140 works by no less than fifty-five amazing poets writing in a variety of forms--all inspired by feelings born in the darkest of times.

They express the pain associated with unrequited or all-consuming love gone wrong, as well as where the resulting emotions can take us. Readers will get in touch with the darkness lurking inside all of us—the ugly part of us—where we can consider the unthinkable, stemming from the madness gripping our minds.

Beautiful Tragedies Vol II

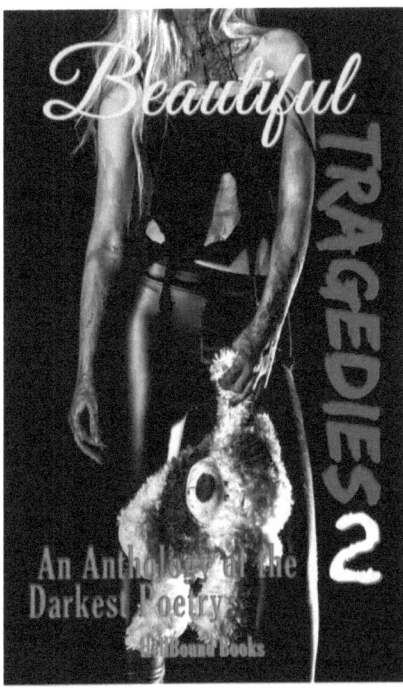

40 amazing poets come together to create one beautifully tragic anthology!

Join us in celebrating the wonderfully macabre and tragically beautiful world of dark poetry, where love isn't always hearts and flowers and that noise you heard—well, we would strongly advise you against going to investigate.

Here, for your blood-curdling entertainment, are over 100 poems written by an amazingly diverse group of poets—including a Bram Stoker award winner, Amazon best-selling horror authors, and our very own Dark Poet Princess—who know poetry can be so much more than lovely, lyrical sentences strung together.

Sometimes life is ugly and causes us to bleed terrible words onto tear-soaked scraps of paper in the dead of the night. But... it's always beautifully tragic.

Beautiful Tragedies Vol III

Back by popular demand, Beautiful Tragedies Vol III takes us on a deliciously disturbing journey with all your favorite forms of poetry in this third anthology! 48 amazing poets take on some very dark topics and come together to share their love for the beautiful craft of poetry, proving to the world that even in the darkest of circumstances, there is beauty even in the tragedies.

Dark Musings
Xtina Marie

"Poetry that jumps off the page and squeezes your heart. I loved every word." -New York Times bestselling author, Alessandra Torre.

The dark side of Xtina Marie's poetry delves into intense emotions: heartache, loss, hurt, pain, rage, and a dangerous consuming love which can drive one insane. Dark Musings is not a collection! The author returned to the centuries old practice of Narrative Poetry—the telling of a story through poetry. If you believe you are brave enough to explore the savage emotions of the human heart; Dark Musings will test your mettle.

<u>All My Not-So-Pretty-Ones</u>
Gerri R. Gray

A deliciously depressing collection of not-so-pretty poems, birthed and nurtured in the bleakest recesses of a woman's tormented soul.

Each one a painful reminder that stars cannot shine without darkness.

Each one a stinging wound that bleeds onto the page with imagery to inspire and help you purge your own personal demons.

New World Monsters
Chris McAuley & Jeff Oliver

Step into a world unlike any other.

A world that is not your own. Or is it?

Here you will find monsters you can see an monsters that you cannot. At the ready to rip your soul apart and open doors that you should have left closed. New World Monsters are coming… RUN!

New World Monsters is a must read for lovers of horror poetry. Jeff Oliver and Chris McAuley speak to us in whispers and screams, weaving dark verses about monsters, pain, and prisons of the mind. Illustrated by the nightmarish visions of Dan Verkys, this collection will send cold shivers down your back.
--Owl Goingback, Bram Stoker Award-Winning author of Crota & Coyote Rage

"New World Monsters is a towering masterclass of narrative poetry, a trip through Lovecraftian macabre by two connoisseurs of the dark fantastic."
—Brandon Scott, author of Vodou

"Chris McCauley and Jeff Oliver's New World Monsters is pure metal, featuring page after page of dark poetry telling tales of monsters all too human, pouring out personal pain from the depths of their tortured souls, punctuated by the glorious, and haunting visual images crafted by the incredibly talented Dan Veryks," – Sumiko Saulson, Ladies of Horror Fiction Readers Choice Award Winning Author of Within Me Without Me

"Raw, transgressive and unrelenting, *New World Monsters* is a hellish journey into Lovecraftian madness and mayhem. Stitched together with Dan Verkys' striking and sinister art, this collection by Jeff Oliver and Chris McAuley drags readers into the depths of the abyss and slices open its black heart, spilling forth every nightmarish vision inside."
—Geneve Flynn
Bram Stoker Award®-winning editor and author of Black Cranes: Tales of Unquiet Women & Tortured Willows: Bent, Bowed, Unbroken

**A HellBound Books LLC
Publication 2025**

www.hellboundbooks.com

Printed in the United States of America